THE
LAST
ORPHANS

BY: N.W. HARRIS

Clean Teen Publishing

THE LAST ORPHANS

ISBN: 978-1-940534-89-3
Cover Design by: Marya Heiman
Typography by: Courtney Nuckels
Editing by: Cynthia Shepp

For more information about our content disclosure, please utilize the QR code above with your smart phone or visit us at

www.CleanTeenPublishing.com.

CHAPTER ONE

Dad twisted away from the steering wheel and glared, the veins in his leathery neck and temple bulging.

"You can't keep carrying on about it, Shane," he yelled. "She's dead! That's the short and sweet."

"Bill! Look where you're going!" Jackie, his dad's girlfriend, put one hand on the roof and one on the dash, bracing for a collision.

Spinning forward, Dad jerked the wheel. The tires screeched, and the car veered into its lane. Shane's six-foot-tall body whipped hard to the left, and then right, his head slamming into the upper part of the doorframe with a loud thunk. A lifted four-wheel drive almost flattened the ancient station wagon. It swerved toward the opposite shoulder, roaring by with its horn blaring and the driver hanging his finger out at them. Cursing and rubbing the lump growing on the side of his skull, Shane almost wished the truck had put him out of his misery.

By the time Dad got his window down and hurled a

1 ➤ N.W. Harris

mouthful of slurred insults back at the truck, it was already a quarter mile down the road.

"Such a tough guy," Shane muttered under his breath.

"What did you say, boy?" Dad shouted, his knuckles white from gripping the steering wheel so hard. At least this time, he kept his eyes forward.

"Nothing," Shane replied and looked out at the rolling hills covered in brown fescue, pastures separated by stands of twisted pine trees and rusting barbwire.

Jackie lit a Virginia Slim with trembling hands. She took a deep drag and rolled her window down a crack to pull out some of the disgusting smoke.

"You have got to be the worst driver alive," she seethed between puffs.

"Well, it's that one's fault," Dad retorted with a defensive whine in his tone, like he always did when she laid into him. Pointing his thumb at the backseat, he glared at Shane in the rearview mirror, the car drifting across the centerline again. "You still cry'n?"

Shane was, but it wasn't like he sobbed inconsolably. Silent tears clung in his eyes for two very good reasons. One—Shane loved Granny. She was the sanest person in his jacked-up family. She had always been there when he needed a place to run to, a place where he could find a minute of peace. And now she was gone. It felt like a round bale of hay—those big ones full of moldy thistle they fed to cattle—sat on his chest. Reason two—Shane's boiling anger towards his dad made him want to punch something. With each passing moment, the pressure of his bottled-up rage increased. Dad getting drunk and being a prick to him in private was one thing. Spewing so much crap about Granny at the reception—for that, he deserved to have his nose busted. And he didn't even have the decency to wear a suit to the funeral, showing up in his greasy, blue work Dickies with his stupid name above the shirt pocket.

Dad slammed on the brakes and swerved off onto the shoulder. Gravel tinged against the corroded bottom of the musty, old car, and a cloud of dust engulfed it as it skidded to a halt. He jumped out and ran around the front to get to Shane's door, leaning over so he could glower at him the whole way. He pulled it open so hard that it was a miracle it didn't come off its creaking, thirty-year-old hinges.

"Get the hell out!"

Shane stared up at him, unsure how to proceed.

"I said get out, damn it," Dad repeated, spittle flying from his mouth. "I won't have a sixteen-year-old boy bawl'n like a little girl all the way home. Man up or walk."

Too much wine had left Dad's teeth and lips stained red, and Shane could smell the alcohol, even over the foul stench of Jackie's cigarette. His aunt had whispered an apology to Shane at the funeral reception, saying she'd only put wine out because she didn't think his dad would drink it. What she didn't realize was Dad had become such a raging alcoholic that he would've drunk turpentine if it were on the table.

His father's eyes widened, and his fists balled up. Shane thought he would grab him and try to drag him from the car.

"You know what?" Shane shouted. Gritting his teeth,

he climbed out. He had grown a lot in the last two years; he wasn't the little boy scared of the big man anymore. Speaking quieter, Shane put all the meanness he could into each word, "I hate your stupid car."

Standing there with his arms crossed over his chest, Shane stared down at his father's sunburned baldhead. Dad pulled his oil-stained hand away from the door and straightened up in an obvious attempt to be taller. He huffed, his breath smelling like another DUI in the making.

Was he daring Shane to hit him? *Why not? It might do him some good*, Shane thought. And if he could knock him out, he'd be keeping him from driving drunk. It'd be a community service.

Dad leaned back. The whiskers of his thick, red-and-gray mustache pulled down on the sides and twitched. The muscles in his forearms, swollen from twenty years of work as a mechanic, rippled. His big, scarred knuckles protruded outward as his fists clenched tighter. Shane braced himself. He'd taken a thousand hits on the football field; he could handle one from this old man.

"Don't come home 'til you're done blubber'n," Dad growled with faltering bravado.

"I wasn't planning on it," Shane replied, slamming the door so hard the car's decrepit suspension complained with loud, reverberating squeaks.

Dad hesitated and then he pivoted away, stomping back around the front of the car. He hopped in and must've floored the accelerator, because the engine groaned for a moment, threatening to stall. With a noxious puff of black exhaust, it roared to life and spun the rear tires in the dusty gravel on the side of the road.

Shane turned away and covered his face just in time. Once the rocks stopped pelting him, he picked one up and threw it with all his strength at the smoke and dirt cloud into which the car disappeared. Dust stinging his eyes and nose, he stumbled away from the road to get out of the choking plume and fell. Rolling to a stop at the bottom of the ditch, he lay there on his back in his Sunday finest.

Granny bought him the black suit to wear on special occasions, getting it a little on the big side so he'd get use out of it for a few years. She'd be sad to see it abused like this. It upset Shane something fierce. He felt more important when he wore the suit, felt like he was going places, like he could escape Loserville and see the world. Of course his dad had to ruin it, just like he ruined everything else.

After Shane calmed down and caught his breath, he decided it felt good just to lie there on the cool ground for a minute. Granny had always loved dirt, saying it strengthened her connection to God when she touched it. She liked to walk barefoot around her small garden where she grew most of her food. He remembered sitting next to her on the strip of grass that grew down the center, listening to crickets and counting the stars. How could he have known Saturday was the last time he'd ever get to do that with her, that she'd be dead two days later?

Biting the side of his tongue and rubbing his nose, Shane suppressed the tears. Granny was in a box, in the dirt, and there wasn't jack he could do about it. The idea of being buried after he died gave Shane the heebie-jeebies, but it didn't bother Granny. On that last night, sitting in the yard, she said she didn't even need a coffin, that she'd rather have the cool soil right up against her skin. It was like she knew she'd die soon, even though she seemed more fit than Shane at the time.

Against Granny's wishes, his aunt flew in from New York, bought the finest box she could afford, and spent a mint on the reception. He knew it was just her way of doing something nice for Granny, but he wished she hadn't provided booze. Dad wouldn't have acted like such an idiot if it weren't for the wine. In this small town, it seemed everyone knew everything about everyone else. Shane expected the commotion Dad created would be popular gossip for the next few months.

Before, when Dad was being a jerk, Shane would go to Granny's house. She'd feed him some fried green tomatoes and buttermilk biscuits the size of a cat's head, or sometimes a fresh cucumber sandwich, and listen to him vent until he'd calmed down. Then he'd help her in the garden or they'd play board games, until Dad sobered up and called sounding all apologetic, on the downside of one of his rollercoaster rides.

Standing up and making a futile attempt at brushing his suit clean, Shane wished he could go to Granny now. The smoldering heat called for a few glasses of her sweet iced tea. He took off his jacket and his light blue, clip-on tie and hung them over his arm, cursing at the sight of a tear in the left sleeve.

He'd been dropped off in front of a creepy, kudzu-covered lot. The vines blanketed a deserted structure so completely that he couldn't tell if it was a house or a barn. The kudzu also engulfed a couple of trees, making them look like giant, green ghosts looming on either side of the unidentifiable building, warning all to stay clear. Shane heard a long time ago that the stuff grew a foot a day. He could almost sense the creepers stretching out toward him, wanting to entangle and strangle him. A hot breeze rustled the kudzu's broad, dusty leaves, and it sounded like the wicked plant was hissing at him. In a hurry to get away from the desolate lot, he started down the side of the pothole-riddled road, heading in the opposite direction Dad had gone.

Might as well stop by Granny's, he decided. There was nowhere else to go. Regular clothes and shoes awaited him there. And he reckoned the fridge still harbored a pitcher of sweet tea. Tears welled up in his eyes knowing she wouldn't be there, and his heart ached realizing how lonely her little, white cottage would feel. An image of her vacant property ten years from now, swallowed by the kudzu, struck him. The thought made his skin crawl and the knots in his gut cinch tighter.

CHAPTER TWO

After the scorching August sun passed its peak, it shined directly into Shane's eyes, making him squint so hard his face hurt. Perspiration soaked his white, button-down shirt and rolled down his cheeks in little streams. The muggy heat demanded shorts and a T-shirt, and the thick, black slacks made his legs feel like two suckling pigs being slow roasted in a barbeque pit. Sweat drenched his stiff, leather dress shoes as well, and his useless polyester socks kept sliding down into them.

Within ten minutes, painful blisters swelled up on Shane's ankles. He stopped in the shade of an old oak tree growing in an empty field alongside the road, its gnarled branches reaching well across the fence. Four miserable miles stood between him and Granny's house, an easier walk if he had his sneakers and if he knew she'd be there to greet him.

He settled on a large clump of grass, crossed his arms over his knees, and rested his head on them. Closing his tired eyes, he contemplated hiding under the protection of the oak for the rest of the day. If he sat there long enough, the sun would be lower, and it would cool a bit. But the low, drawn-out rumble of thunder off in the distance warned he'd better keep moving. They'd had a lightning storm every afternoon for the last month, typical for North Georgia in the late summer. The rain would feel good, but he doubted his slacks and dress shoes would be any easier to walk in for it. And he didn't relish the idea of being struck by lightning, a likely occurrence if he stayed out here in the open and even more probable if he sat under the tree for too long.

An ominous humming caught his attention, and Shane looked up to see a beach-ball-size hornets' nest engulfing several branches about ten-feet overhead. The black-and-gold hornets were three times as big as a normal wasp, and they looked angry, buzzing around as if someone had thrown a rock at them. Shane stiffened. He'd been stung by one of the massive insects once when he was little, and it had left a welt as big as a golf ball on his arm that took weeks to heal. He slowly rose to a crouch and slipped out of the shade of the tree, not daring to breathe until he was twenty feet away. Once he no longer heard the threatening drone of their beating wings, he stopped and glanced back.

They acted crazy agitated, swarming around the oak's canopy in a threatening way. A stray one buzzed past his ear and he ducked, then turned and hurried down the road, not risking another look.

After a few minutes, the adrenaline wore off, and the heat made Shane worry less about the hornets. His pace slackened. He gave up on walking on the gravelly shoulder, finding limited relief for his blistered ankles on the flat surface of the asphalt. Shane raised his hand, attempting to shield his face from the blistering sun, though even more heat seemed to be reflecting off the blacktop.

A sudden roar came from behind him, accompanied by the blare of an air horn. Shane leapt off the road onto the shoulder, hurdled over the ditch, and then landed next to the fence. A semi loaded with ill-fated chickens barreled by in a blast of wind, no doubt headed for the processing plant. It disappeared around the corner, leaving the grass dancing and little, white feathers floating down in the black diesel smoke of its wake.

Shane's pulse raced from the near miss. In his rush to get out of the big rig's way, he'd almost fallen onto the heavy gage electric fence containing the Douglas' pasture. Down the hill, he saw the cattle stampeding around in a peculiar way. Usually, during this hottest part of the day, they would find shelter under a tree or wade in the stagnant water of their pond. Instead, they ran in wide circles as though a pack of wild mutts nipped at their heels, but he didn't hear any barking and couldn't see a single dog. They came up the hill and charged at the thick, aluminum cables of the fence, heading straight for Shane with such fury that he expected they would plow through it and trample him. He tensed, ready to sprint across the road and jump in the opposite ditch, but the cattle changed direction abruptly and headed the other way, down the hill toward the barns.

Stunned, Shane watched the herd rumble away. He figured a few would die of heatstroke if someone didn't calm them soon. Because Kelly Douglas—the hottest girl in the twelfth grade and his future wife when hogs learned to fly—might answer, he entertained the temptation to go down to the palatial farmhouse and knock on the door to offer his assistance. A glance at his sweaty, dirt-covered clothing made him decide against it. He'd have to make the varsity team before he'd have a chance with Kelly anyway. Not to mention, it was unlikely she'd give a junior the time of day. And there wasn't much he could do to help with the cattle dressed like this.

Thunder boomed, and mountainous purple clouds moved in from the west. The wind started to blow harder, and he hurried down the road with more haste. The approaching storm must've been putting the cattle on edge. Shane knew that sometimes animals acted rash before a tornado struck. The notion of being stranded outside in a twister put even more speed in his pace.

Not more than ten minutes had passed before a rustling sound in the deep grass on the left side of the road startled Shane again. Hundreds of rats leapt out of the ditch and scampered onto the scorched asphalt a few feet in front of him, stopping his progress. They paused in unison and all turned their beady eyes toward him, raising their noses and twitching their whiskers as if to smell him. A sudden rush of fear caused him to freeze. Before he had a chance to take a step back from the abnormally bold rodents, they continued on, vanishing as quickly as they appeared into the cornfield on the other side of the road. Angry hornets, stampeding cattle, and now this—one heck of a storm was surely brewing. Or, he feared, the heat was getting to him, and he was starting to hallucinate.

The sky took on a light green hue, a sickly color that preceded really nasty weather. With a mile and a half to go until he made it to Granny's house, Shane started a limping sort of jog, knowing he'd better get into her cellar soon or he could be in big trouble. Sharp pain exploded in his feet and ankles with each step, and he expected half of the moisture in his shoes might be blood. He didn't dare stop and look, knowing the pain would only get worse once he exposed his ruptured blisters to air.

The sound of an engine downshifting behind him made him run off onto the shoulder. The car's horn beeped, and he turned to see his aunt's rental slowing down as it approached. Relief flooded through him, and his legs suddenly felt too rubbery to keep him upright.

"What in heaven's name are you doing out here?" his aunt asked once she came alongside him. Her eyes were red and moist, likely from crying over her mother's death.

"Dad kicked me out," he replied, immediately wishing he'd lied and said he just thought it was a nice day for a stroll.

"Oh Shane, I'm sorry to hear that," she said with an unsurprised, though compassionate tone. Smiling kindly, she had the decency not to pursue the issue. "You'd better get in, looks like we're in for some inclement weather."

"It does, don't it?" he said, rushing around to the passenger side.

"Where are you heading?" she asked once he'd climbed into the car and buckled his seatbelt. She didn't have the thick, southern accent everyone else Shane knew did, having escaped hickville to go to Yale just after she'd graduated from high school. She sounded so proper and intelligent to him.

"Granny's," he replied, leaning closer to the air conditioning vent and peeling the saturated, button-down shirt away from his chest to dry it.

His aunt gazed thoughtfully at him for a long moment, her sad, brown eyes so much like his mother's that it made his chest ache. "That's where I was going too." She shifted the car into gear. "I have to help settle her estate before I return to New York."

It was hard not to stare at his aunt while she drove; she reminded him so much of his mom. She had the same wavy, black hair, pointed nose, and always-tan skin. But his aunt had a more sophisticated and well-traveled air about her. Shane had always been in awe of her and found it hard to talk to her because he felt ignorant and backwoods in her presence. Wisps of gray twisted through her hair now that he didn't remember seeing when she visited last Christmas. He wondered if his mother would have some too if she were still around—though his aunt was two years older than his mom, who would've been forty-five this year.

She glanced over, and he looked out the window. His mother's death still hurt like it happened yesterday. Adding the pain from losing Granny made him expect he'd never smile again. *How the heck do people ever get over stuff like this?* he wondered. Maybe they never did. Maybe they just acted like they did because it was what was expected.

The car weaved through the curviest part of Rural Route 2. He always felt a little carsick when he passed through here.

"You've grown so much since the last time I saw you," she said. "You look just like your grandfather."

It was a nice compliment; the pictures he'd seen of the wiry Green Beret soldier impressed him. Granny said he was a stern man who didn't smile much, and Shane reckoned his grandfather must've seen some things in the wars he'd fought that would kill the joy in anyone.

"He was tall, with a darker complexion too. You have his brown eyes and his dimpled chin." She retrieved a green, glass bottle from the center console and took a sip of water from it, and then offered it to him. "Good thing. Not to sound rude, but I never thought your dad was overly handsome."

"It's okay," Shane replied, graciously accepting the bottle. "I'd have to agree with you. Dad's not much of a looker." The carbonated water tasted bitter, but he was parched. Not wanting to look unsophisticated, he tried not to grimace after taking a sip.

He wished he had met his grandfather. Granny told Shane lots of stories about him. He was a real, live war hero— had even won the Congressional Medal of Honor in Vietnam.

"It must be hard for you, losing your mom and now Granny," his aunt said distantly.

Tears flooded Shane's eyes again. He nodded and looked out of the window, so his aunt couldn't see his face. He was used to being strong and stoic around everyone except his grandmother, and his aunt's pity made him uncomfortable.

"You know I'm always here for you if you want to talk," she said. "You can call me anytime."

"Thanks," Shane replied.

He wished he could talk to her, now more than ever before, but he couldn't relax around his aunt, no matter how hard he tried. The closest they'd ever been was that night in the hospital, when his mom passed. Since then, he and his aunt hadn't really bonded. Loneliness settled over him, a dark cloud pressing him down into his seat.

His aunt chuckled. "Remember that time when—" She cursed and slammed on the brakes, turning the wheel hard to the left.

Shane glanced up at a fat dairy cow standing in the middle of the road. The little rental car's tires screeched, and it slid at an angle toward the animal. The car slammed into the cow with a sickening thud and a metallic crunching sound. Split seconds seemed long as minutes, and the hood pressed into the animal. Then, its soft belly rebounded as the sharp metal made an incision. Shockwaves emanated from the impact, rippling across the flesh of the cow's hip and shoulder. Its head whipped toward the car, and then away, its dark, blue-black eye wide with shock. The hood folded as Shane's face approached the windshield. Time made a sudden return to the normal pace, and the seatbelt punched into his chest. The airbag exploded with the sound of a shotgun going off, smashing Shane back into his seat.

Chapter Three

"Oh my God," his aunt gasped. She looked over at Shane. "Are you okay?"

"I think so," he replied hoarsely, having trouble getting air. "But your nose is bleeding."

She wiped it and studied the blood on the back of her hand, stunned. Her eyes widened, and her tan skin turned whiter than he'd ever seen it.

"Here," Shane said, handing her the handkerchief he had stuffed in his inside jacket pocket.

She held it to her nose, and they climbed out. Blood covered the car's crumpled front end. Jagged bits of bone, burst organs, and shredded meat lay in a quivering pile entangled in the front bumper. Shane stared down at the twisted carnage, his body shivering from the shock of the accident. What was left of the cow's legs twitched, and its mouth opened and closed like it struggled to take a breath.

His aunt had her phone out. "I'm calling 911," she said frantically, turning her back to the wreck. The howling wind whipped her hair into a rat's nest and made it hard for

Shane to hear her.

Shane couldn't stop looking at the dying cow. He wanted to do something to help but didn't know where to start. Its crimson blood flowed across the hot asphalt toward him, mixing with neon-green radiator fluid trickling out of the car. He inched back so it wouldn't get on his dusty, leather dress shoes.

"Come on, come on," his aunt said, "why isn't anyone answering?"

It may have been a minute or five before the cow stopped trying to live and lay still. But to Shane, watching and imagining how much suffering the poor animal was enduring, it seemed like a torturous eternity. Pacing back and forth on the other side of the car, his aunt dialed again and held the phone to her ear. Shane tore his eyes away from the dead animal. The metallic smell of blood mixed with the chemically smell of the car's fluids started his head spinning. He stumbled to the rear of the car and put his hand on the trunk. Leaning over so he wouldn't get any on his clothes, he waited for the vomit to come up.

"Are you sure you're okay, sweetie?" His aunt walked around and put a trembling hand on his shoulder, the other still holding the phone to her ear. Her voice had a hysterical pitch, like she was about to lose control.

"Yeah," Shane lied. Too dizzy to stand, he squatted down. The hot, tar smell rising from the asphalt didn't help his nausea. "I'm fine. Just a little shaken up."

"911 isn't answering," she said worriedly. "I've tried three times, and it just keeps ringing and ringing."

"Maybe we should call the police station directly," Shane suggested, pulling out his phone.

"You have the number?" she asked, incredulous.

"Granny made me put all the emergency numbers in my phone," he replied.

"Sounds like her," she said with a weak grin and leaned back against the car's trunk, putting his handkerchief up to her nose.

Shane dialed the number for the police. After twenty rings and no answer, he tried the fire department. No one there either.

"That's so odd." His aunt crossed her arms over her chest and hunched forward, looking ill.

"A tornado might've struck town," Shane said, studying the horizon to the west. The sky was still the eerie lime color, and the wind blew even harder now.

"You may be right. We should get to Granny's house." His aunt surveyed the front of the car, its tires twisted out at opposite angles. "I don't think we'll be able to drive."

"It's only about a half mile from here," Shane replied, trying to keep his eyes from drifting back down to the twisted carnage. "We can walk."

He hooked his arm through his aunt's. They started down the road, leaning forward and shielding their faces against the dirt and dust the wind whipped up. She looked so awkward and delicate with her fancy, black dress, high heels, and expensive purse tucked under her arm. Being a city person, she seemed as skittish and out of place here in the middle of nowhere as a horse in a henhouse.

They passed the sprawling walnut tree Granny said her father planted when she was born, and the wind died down. The electrified quiet made Shane worry a twister would strike at any second. He eyed the drainage ditch, knowing they could take refuge in it if need be, or even crawl into one of the large, concrete pipes running under the road if things got really bad.

"This is way too creepy," his aunt said and walked faster. "This is why I'll take New York over Georgia any day."

"Do you hear that?" Shane asked. A deep humming caught his attention. He glanced back, but he didn't see anything.

"Yes, weird. But at this point, I don't care to find out what it is." She kicked her shoes off and started jogging on her panty hose-covered feet. "We just need to get to shelter."

Shane jogged beside her, and the humming grew into a near-deafening drone. Off to the left, he saw a dark cloud moving straight toward them, hovering a few feet above the dry, brown grass in the pasture. Horror gripping him, his skin tingled from head to toe.

"Hornets!" he shouted.

"What?" his aunt asked.

"Run!"

CHAPTER FOUR

Shane grabbed his aunt's hand and pulled her along as fast as he could. The dark cloud closed in, and he saw individual insects buzzing ahead of him. He noticed more than hornets in the swarm. He saw several kinds of wasps, yellow jackets, and honeybees as well—like everything with a stinger and wings joined forces to chase them.

"I've been stung!" His aunt screamed and slapped at her head.

"We can't slow down," Shane yelled over the sound of a million tiny wings beating the air.

She screamed again and flailed her free arm, swatting at the bees. Shane glanced over and saw several of the massive, shiny, black-and-yellow hornets on her chest and neck. A wall of angry bugs towered behind, a giant wave about to crash on top of them. A hot surge of fear prodding him to a sprint, he turned onto the packed, red clay of Granny's driveway. His aunt tripped and fell, her hand jerking out of his grasp.

Spinning on his heel, Shane dove down to scoop her up, and the dark cloud of bees engulfed them. It sounded like he'd stuck his head into a jet engine's intake, and he couldn't see a thing. He cringed, expecting thousands of stingers to pierce him at once. He felt the heat created by the swarm and could barely hear his aunt screaming in agony as they stung her. Holding his breath to keep from sucking the bugs into his lungs, he reached down and patted the ground. Finding his aunt's leg, he moved his hands up her body, which felt encased in a writhing fur jacket. A thick layer of bees covered every inch of her skin. Terror turned his blood to ice, but adrenaline spurred him into action. He scooped her up, threw her over his shoulder like a sack of feed, and charged on in the direction in which he guessed Granny's house lay.

Leaping free of the deadly cloud just as he made it to the steps of the front porch, Shane gasped for air, rushed up, and pulled open the screen. The door was locked. The swarm closed in on him again, blocking out the light. Shane leaned back and kicked with all his strength. The jamb exploded into splinters, and the door slammed inward. Rushing into the house, he elbowed the door shut behind him. He lowered his aunt to the floor and then used a chair to prop the door closed.

His aunt rolled back and forth, swatting and wailing. Hundreds of wasps and bees clung to her, their bodies curled up so they could inject their venom. Louder than the noise of her screams, Shane's pulse banged in his ears, his head seeming to swell. He picked some insects off and stomped on them, but he knew she'd die before he could save her with just his hands. The ones he didn't manage to squash flew back onto her and sank their stingers in again. Desperate to find a way to help her, he scooped his aunt up and took her into the bathroom. He stood her in the shower, turned the water on, and tried to wash the bees away.

"Please make them stop!" his aunt yelled, thrashing around so much he had trouble keeping her in the tub.

"I'm trying, Aunt Lillian," he replied, his voice choked with terror, "but you have to be still."

Shane grabbed a stack of towels from the cabinet and wet them, using the towels to wipe the bees from his aunt's skin. The shower curtain tangled around his arm and he jerked to break free, bringing the rod down on his head. Cursing, he slung the curtain aside and the rod slammed into the vanity mirror behind him, shattering it into a million shards that fell around his feet. Dripping with sweat from the effort, he used the wet towels to bury the bees in the tub. After an arduous half hour with his aunt shrieking in agony the entire time, Shane managed to free her of the last of the vicious insects. When he wrapped her in Granny's bathrobe, she collapsed in his arms and he lifted her out of the tub.

Her face was swelled up as if she'd been beaten with a baseball bat, and her arms looked twice as thick as they should.

"Shane," she wheezed, "I can't see." Her eyelids were swelled closed, and her bright red face oozed blood from all the holes the stingers created. "My whole body feels like it's on fire."

"It's going to be okay," he said, the words sticking in his throat.

If she puffed up any more, he feared she might explode. He'd never seen anyone with so many stings, and he couldn't imagine how she could survive. She needed to see a doctor, and quick, or he knew she would die.

Tears blurred his vision, and he carried her into the bedroom and laid her on the bed, trying not to think about Granny dying there just days before. Rushing into the kitchen, he grabbed the phone and dialed 911. It rang and rang, but no one picked up.

"Please—somebody answer, damn it," he whispered into the receiver, dizzy with panic. After a minute, he dialed zero to see if he could even get an operator. With no answer still, he went back in to check on his aunt, worried she was running out of time.

She looked even worse than before. Massive red-and-purple welts, most of them bleeding, covered her face, ears, lips, arms, and every exposed part of her body. She shivered violently, and her breaths came short and harsh.

"You all right, Aunt Lillian?" He used a finger to clear her wet, black-and-gray hair from her face. Her eyes and smile had always reminded him of his mother, but now she was unrecognizable. She barely looked human.

She moaned a feeble response. Shane attempted to check the pulse at her wrist and then her neck, as he'd learned to do in CPR class for his part-time summer job as a lifeguard at the county pool. Her lumpy flesh made it impossible to find, and his fingers left sickening indentations in her skin when he removed them.

Smothered by dread, Shane rushed to the front door and pulled back the curtain hanging over the small, diamond-shaped window. A thick layer of bees obscured the glass, crawling around and searching for a way in. They assailed all the other windows in the house as well, and it grew darker as more joined the swarm. Cold fear rushed through Shane's veins. Had every bee and wasp in the county converged on Granny's house?

A wasp buzzed past his ear and he smacked it to the floor, stomping it with a vengeance. It suddenly occurred to him he hadn't been stung once. How was it possible? His aunt suffered hundreds, if not thousands, of stings, and he was right next to her, had even held her in his arms and smashed some of the insects against his skin. Something strange and unnatural was happening, but he couldn't begin to guess what.

The keys to Granny's old Ford Ranger hung on the rack by the front door. Shane snatched them and rushed to the garage, praying her beloved truck was inside. The garage was dark and stuffy, the windows blanketed with hornets. A couple made it in and buzzed threateningly around the truck.

A sharp sigh of relief hissed between his clenched teeth. He'd drive his aunt to the hospital, and they would save her. Latching onto the measure of hope, he ran back to the bedroom in such a hurry that he slammed into a doorjamb, the dishes rattling in the china cabinet on the other side of the wall.

"Don't you worry, Aunt Lillian," he said, rubbing his shoulder and wincing from the sobering pain. He tried to sound encouraging. "We're gonna get you to a doctor."

She didn't move or make a sound, and he feared her body had lost its fight against the massive dose of venom. Leaning close to her puffy, red face, he could hear her wheezing with each labored breath. She sounded like she wouldn't make it for much longer—sounded a lot like the cow they'd hit right before it died.

Shocked by how hot her skin felt, he lifted her in his arms. Shane carried her through the house and into the garage, turning sideways so as not to bump her head or swollen feet against the doors and walls. He could hear the insects buzzing around outside, wanting to come in and finish his aunt off.

"Not today, damn it," he growled, anger surging.

Laying his aunt on the seat, he smacked a wasp flying into the cab after her. He ran around, climbed in, and jabbed the key in the ignition with such force that he cut his finger on the chrome ridge surrounding the keyhole. When he jerked his hand away, the silver chain with a cross on it hanging from the ring wrapped around his hand and the keys came flying out, landing on the passenger floorboard.

Shane cursed and leaned over to retrieve the key. His aunt let out a weak moan when he pressed against her, and he knew he had to calm down or he'd never get her to the hospital. He let out a slow and shaky breath, reinserted the key in the ignition, and twisted it.

The small block 302 roared to life, and Shane was grateful he'd done a tune-up on the engine two weeks earlier. It would get them to the hospital in a hurry without issue. After a last check to ensure the windows were rolled up tight, he said a silent prayer and clicked the garage door opener. Bees spilled in under the aluminum door as it rose, engulfing the truck.

Shane turned on the windshield wipers and smeared

insects across the glass. Hoping he could kill even more, he floored the accelerator. The rear tires squealed on the greasy, concrete floor. When the tires bit, the truck charged out of the garage and down the driveway with the engine roaring.

By the time he turned on Rural Route 2, heading east toward town and the hospital, his aunt started having a seizure. She flopped around on the seat next to him, punching him and kicking the passenger door so hard that he expected it might fly open. Shane pressed his right arm over her to keep her on the seat and struggled to keep the truck on the road.

"Please hold on, Aunt Lillian," Shane begged, tears making it even harder to see through the bug-gut-covered windshield.

Shane glanced in the rearview mirror and saw that hornets blanketed the back window. Sick with terror, he pushed the truck harder, the speedometer rising above eighty. The tires left the ground at the top of a hill, and they screeched around the bend at the western corner of the Douglas' farm.

His aunt stopped bucking and kicking, and she stiffened as if every muscle in her body contracted at once. Shane's heart rose into his throat, and hot tears spilled down his cheeks.

"Aunt Lillian!" Shane shouted. "Don't give up on me! You hear me, damn it?"

She didn't move. Shane couldn't breathe.

"You'll be alright," Shane said, sniffling. "I'm not gonna to let you die." He used a fist to wipe his eyes and then gripped the steering wheel so hard his knuckles cracked. Shaking his head in defiance, he pushed the accelerator into the floorboard.

"We're going to the hospital—they'll have you fixed up in no time."

He feared he was only lying to himself at this point, that she was already dead and he was rushing her corpse to the morgue. But he couldn't be certain—she might just be unconscious. He had to drive faster, had to get her to help.

Shane steered the truck around the hairpin blind turn at the Douglas' driveway and came out of it with the dual exhaust pipes and the rear tires belching white smoke. Up ahead, he saw a massive, dark box blocking the road. The Ranger barreled toward a tractor-trailer flipped over onto its side. His eyes went wide and he slammed both feet onto the brake pedal, pulling the wheel hard to the right. The old pickup slid sideways, rocked up onto two tires, and slammed into the belly of the rig. The window on his door exploded, glass pelting his face and landing in his lap.

Stunned, Shane took a quick account of himself. Other than the painful bruise on his shoulder from running into the doorjamb at Granny's house, he seemed uninjured. The engine stalled, and only the clicking sound of cooling metal punctuated the morbid silence. Realizing he didn't have a window to keep the hornets out, Shane jerked his head around to see outside of the cab. He expected insects to swarm in, but they had vanished. Not a single wasp buzzed around the truck.

Aunt Lillian lay motionless next to him, looking asleep. Leaning over, Shane put his ear by her mouth and his fingers where he thought her carotid artery should be. No air flowed in and out of her, and he couldn't feel a pulse.

"No, please," he gasped, acidic bile burning his throat.

Lifting her chin and blowing into her lungs, the metallic taste of blood on her engorged lips drew vomit up into the back of his mouth. Swallowing hard and trying to stay focused, he compressed her chest thirty times and blew two more breaths into her. He kept doing CPR until sweat burned his eyes and her ribs cracked under his palms with each compression. His arms went rubbery, and spots swam in his vision. Shane leaned against the dash to keep from collapsing. Panting, he stared down at her. Her tan skin had turned a pale gray color, and her swollen tongue protruded between her lips.

Silent tears welled in his eyes and spilled down his cheeks. He cried for her, for Granny, and for his mother. Death stole too much from him. Fresh anger erupted in tiny fires throughout his body, growing into an inferno that made him grit his teeth and caused a red haze to close in on his vision.

He slammed his right fist into the roof of the truck. Bits of the insulation exposed by rips in the old headliner rained down from the impact. Following with a left fist, the sheet metal reported a loud thunk and more of the crumbling headliner fell. He threw another right fist, punching again and again, yelling until his throat hurt. When his arms gave out, refusing to push his bruised knuckles up into the ceiling of the cab anymore, he collapsed and hugged his aunt in his arms. Sobbing into her damp, black hair, Shane's voice was hoarse as he begged her to wake up. Pressing her tight against his chest, he tried to will life back into her limp body.

She was dead. Gone forever.

CHAPTER FIVE

Light faded from the gloomy heavens as Shane climbed over his aunt and out of the passenger side of the cab. Ominous green clouds still choked the sky, but the air was calm and quiet. He walked a few yards away and turned around, staring absently at the wreckage and wanting to die. The truck door hung open, his aunt's swollen feet sticking out. Crippling numbness overtook him, pressing in on all sides, as if he were being buried in wet cement. It invaded his mind, drowning his thoughts, and leaving only dejected questions that no one could answer. What was he supposed to do now? Why did he have to still be alive when everyone he loved was being taken from him?

"Help!" A girl's hysterical voice ripped through his viscous daze like a bullet through a soda can. "Can you please? Help!"

The voice was pitched with agony and grief, but also very familiar.

Shane pivoted, the weight of his aunt's nightmarish demise making it hard to move.

Two girls ran up the Douglas' long, gravel driveway toward him. The taller one's tangled, blonde hair billowed behind her. She wore cutoff blue jeans and a baggy, white T-shirt with crimson paint smeared across her chest. She dragged a shorter version of herself by the hand behind her as she ran. It took a second for Shane to register who it was.

"Kelly?" he shouted, his voice hoarse with shock. Struggling to break free of the catatonic state threatening to turn him into stone, he jogged heavily down the driveway to meet her.

"They killed my dad and my mom!" she shrieked, her eyes wild and her gaze darting like she expected some horror to jump out of the fields and attack her. "They went berserk and trampled them!"

"Wait—slow down." Shane grabbed her shoulders to steady her. Her distress tore his mind away from the despair seeping through every part of his body, starving him for breath and welding his joints together. "Who killed your parents?" He realized the red on her clothes was fresh blood.

"The cows," she cried, collapsing into him. "Dad went out in the pasture to herd them into a paddock, and they killed him." She hugged Shane, pressing her face into his shirt and weeping.

Kelly's little sister looked up at Shane, her tear-streaked face slack with confusion and grief.

"What about your mom?" Shane whispered, afraid to hear the answer.

"She was standing by the fence," Kelly replied without taking her face out of his shirt. "After they got Dad, they turned and ran through the wire like it wasn't even there. It was horrible. Then the dogs attacked my grandfather and killed him too."

Kelly leaned back and looked up at him with wide, wet eyes. "Why is this happening, Shane?"

"I don't know." He looked down the hill at the Douglas' farmhouse. Wretched bewilderment coiled around him, a python tightening its grip for the kill. "Something's gone wrong, bad wrong."

"What should we do?"

Having been content with dying moments before, Shane's mind hadn't come to the answer yet. He didn't have a clue. Turning his attention to her bloodshot, wet eyes, he didn't have the heart to tell Kelly that. He stared at her for a long moment, trying to think of something. Scanning the field around them, his gaze stopped on the road.

"We'll have to go to town and see if we can get some help," he said, at a loss for any other ideas.

Putting his arm around Kelly's waist and leaning into her for support almost as much as she leaned into him, he led her up the driveway. The green clouds hung low and heavy overhead, and an ominous bolt of lightning arced beneath them. This was one of the most picturesque stretches of Route 2. It twisted over rolling hills and past the straight, modern fences. Mature oaks separated the fence from the road, allowing a broken view of the green pastures of the Douglas' farm. But at the moment, it looked like Hell on earth.

Shane remembered the pastor at the church his grandmother made him go to preaching about the Book of Revelations, and wondered if this was the beginning of the end. Maybe his aunt and Granny were taken to heaven, spared from the horrible things yet to come. Had he and Kelly been left behind because they weren't good Christians? Had they already sinned so much in their short lives as to incur the wrath of God? If so, why would Kelly's little sister still be here? Shane always understood that the children would be spared in the apocalypse.

"What happened there?" Kelly asked between sobs once they got to the road, pointing at the flipped rig with the brown-and-white Ranger entangled in its undercarriage.

"There was an accident," Shane replied, his voice trembling. "Stay here for a minute. I'll go get the truck." Although she no longer sobbed uncontrollably, tears still streamed down Kelly's face. He didn't want her to see his aunt, figuring it would only make matters worse.

Shane used a tarp he found stowed behind the seat of the truck to cover his aunt's body and then tugged her out of the cab. The bee venom left her swollen and stiff. Her skin felt cold and damp, with fluid leaking from thousands of puncture wounds caused by the stingers. Shane wanted to puke and cry at the same time when he touched her, but he managed to keep it together, knowing he had to help Kelly and her sister.

He cradled his aunt, uncertain what he should do with her body. Leaving it on the side of the road seemed wrong. She wasn't heavy, but Shane's legs grew rubbery and the world began to spin around him. Rushing to get her out of his arms, he lifted her up and lowered her into the back of the truck.

She rolled in and made a horrible thud as she settled onto the metal bed. Guilt adding to his list of torturous emotions, Shane tucked the tarp around her and placed rocks on either side of it so it wouldn't blow off while they drove.

Climbing into the cab from the passenger side, he held his breath and turned the key. To his limited relief, the truck's engine roared to life.

It took a couple of tries, going from reverse to drive, to get the Ranger dislodged from the belly of the semi, and then Shane backed down the road to where Kelly and her sister waited.

"What were you doing?" Kelly asked after she'd climbed in and shut the door. She'd stopped crying, but her eyes were red and moist. Her voice was weak, just audible over the growl of the engine. Her little sister sat in the middle, looking up at Shane with a heartbreaking expression.

"Uh, the truck was stuck against the rig. It took a few minutes to break it free," Shane replied, sensing he didn't answer her question.

"What did you put in the back?" Kelly clarified, slipping the seatbelt around her sister.

"My aunt," he whispered, glancing down at the little girl and back up at Kelly.

Horror flashed through Kelly's blue eyes, but she seemed to understand Shane wanted to spare her sister the details.

Shane steered the truck into the ditch, so they could get around the overturned semi and back up onto Route 2. Coming by the front of the big rig, he caught a glimpse of the cab. Dead crows lay on the ground and dangled from the grill and off the mirrors. The front window of the cab hung in a sheet of thousands of crystals. It reflected the last of the diminishing light, fractured and peeling away from the driver's half of the cab and lying folded across the hood.

Visible through the opening, the driver was limp, suspended by his seatbelt at the same odd angle as the broken windshield. His dripping face hung in shreds, his blood painting the wreckage. A solitary crow perched on the steering wheel, pecking at the holes where the man's eyes should be.

Sick from the sight but still numb from his aunt's horrific death, he looked away from the dead man and focused his eyes on driving. The cushion sank to his right. Kelly's little sister was pushing her hands down into the bench seat, raising herself up to see. He leaned forward to block her view and gunned the pickup onto the asphalt.

Bringing the truck up to speed, he smiled down at the little girl the best he could, hoping to put her at ease. "What's your name?"

She looked up at him for a long moment, her eyes glistening and sad. It seemed hopeless. How could he cheer her up when he was suffering so much inside? She blinked, her lower lip puckering out like she might start bawling, but her eyes stayed fixed upon him and she answered, "I'm Natalie."

"Now that's a pretty name if I've ever heard one," he said, struggling to sound normal and failing miserably.

"It was my mommy's mommy's name." She spoke a

little louder, though so quiet he could just hear her over the engine. Even still, her voice sounded sweet and innocent, like little glass bells ringing.

"That makes it even more special, doesn't it?" Shane replied.

"I guess so." She gave him a feeble grin, and the weight pressing in on his chest seemed to lessen. "Kelly calls me Nat. You can call me Nat too."

"Well, alright." Shane cleared his throat and winked at the girl. "I think I will."

CHAPTER SIX

Five minutes later, they came across another accident. Shane slowed the truck as they approached. A little, red Honda's smashed front end was reaching up a broken telephone pole. At least thirty dogs surrounded it, barking and growling like they'd cornered a coyote. Some stood on the roof and the hood, all their attention focused on whoever sat inside.

Dread washed through Shane. But perhaps he was wrong. There were lots of red Hondas in town. Driving closer, Shane could see her, fighting a dog sticking its head through her window and biting her arm. Her long, blonde hair was painted with blood, glued to her face so she was barely recognizable, but there was little doubt in his mind now. Shane's brow sank over his eyes, and he bit his lip so hard it bled. Without another thought, he aimed the truck at the dogs.

"Don't!" Kelly sounded terrified.

"What?" Shane yelled, the truck twenty yards from the dog-bristled Honda.

"There's nothing you can do, Shane," she said firmly,

pulling Nat into a hug so she couldn't look out. "Please, don't!"

Swallowing the hard lump forming in his throat, Shane pressed the accelerator. He slammed on the brakes as he hit the dogs and the truck smashed at least ten of them, their yelps so loud it made his ears ring. The truck came to a rest a foot from the driver's side door of the wrecked car. The dogs that survived his attack returned their attention to the Honda, climbing onto the hood of the truck to get a better angle on the driver. Her guttural screams carried over the vicious barking and yelping of the dogs.

Shane slammed the truck into park and thrust the door open as hard as he could, batting the dogs on the other side.

"No, Shane!" Kelly yelled.

"I can't just leave her." He jumped out, pushing the door shut behind him so the dogs couldn't get into the cab.

Shane grabbed a big German Sheppard by the skin of its back. He recognized a sticker on the window of the car, and the last bit of doubt as to who was inside vaporized. Mrs. Morris—his best friend's mother. After throwing the dog across the street with all his might, he leapt onto the truck's hood and kicked, punched, and tossed dogs aside, unleashing his bottled rage. They yelped and whined when he hit them, but not a single one tried to bite Shane. They kept pushing their way toward the Honda, toward Mrs. Morris. Over the complaints of the dogs he battled, Shane heard her screams grow weaker.

He made it through the pack of dogs to the car and found a pit bull latched on her neck. Shane punched the dog with all his might in the side of its skull, yet it didn't let go. He straddled the determined animal, crushing in on its ribcage with his knees, and shoved his thumbs into either side of its jaws. Ms. Morris went limp, and the dog's grip relaxed. It jerked and bucked out of Shane's grasp and slid off the hood of the pickup onto the ground.

Like someone flipped a switch, the dogs went from agro to docile. They backed away from the car and sniffed around with their heads hung low, seeming remorseful about having killed the woman.

Shane looked at Mrs. Morris, or what was left of her. A black Labrador pushed its bloody snout under his hand, wagging its tail like it wanted to play. Disgusted, he jerked his arm away and kicked the animal off the hood. He stood alone atop the Ford, his blood boiling as he looked at the dogs. They poked around submissively or sat on their haunches and returned his hateful gaze with innocent eyes and wagging tails—friendly, lost pets that wouldn't harm a soul.

Without warning, they perked up and turned their attention toward the south. They took off barking like they'd seen a rabbit, heading up into the pasture and over the hill. Stupefied to the point of madness, he watched them go.

"Shane," Kelly called from in the truck. "Can we please get out of here?"

His eyes fixed on Mrs. Morris' disfigured and lifeless body in the Honda. She was one of the sweetest people Shane had ever know, always smiling and trying to feed him when he went to Aaron's house. Everyone on the football team thought of her as a second mom, and Coach even let her be on the sidelines during games.

One massive sob rose up from his feet until it encompassed his entire body. A pitiful, jerky sort of yelp came from between his quivering lips, and then he fell silent and motionless, his shoulders drooping and his chin on his chest. A tear burned on his eyelid. The crippling numbness he'd experienced after his aunt died returned, a heavy cloud of gloom smothering his senses and emotions.

"Shane?" Kelly's concerned voice cut through his morbid stupor once again, muffled by the truck's cab. "You alright?"

He tore his eyes away from the corpse and looked down through the windshield. Kelly held Nat's head in her lap, her shirt pulled over the little girl's face so she couldn't see. Kelly's eyes were wide and her skin blanched white. Considering what she'd just seen, her level of composure was a testament to her fierce determination to protect her sister.

Shane glanced back at Ms. Morris and climbed off the hood. How would he tell Aaron? Was he even alive? Getting into the cab, he put the truck in reverse. The Ford rocked left and right. There was a sickening, wet, crunching sound as it rolled back over the dogs he hit on his way in.

Shifting to drive, he steered toward town. Nat whimpered, still lying on Kelly's lap. Shane stared blankly out the windshield, and the violent deaths played over and over in his head as he drove. Each recollection seemed to strip away a chunk of his soul, drawing life out of him.

When he gazed in the rearview mirror, he saw the blue tarp flapping in the truck's bed behind him, his aunt's foot exposed. He slowed down to keep her covered, and to prevent running into any other wrecked cars, which they encountered more frequently as they approached town. The green clouds overhead thickened and blocked the moon. Lightning danced across the sky every few minutes, illuminating the dark and hilly countryside in nightmarish snapshots, and leaving spots swimming in Shane's vision. When he blinked at the glare, the mutilated dead were there—the truck driver with no eyes, his aunt swollen to the point of bursting, and Mrs. Morris bloody and chewed to shreds by the dogs.

"Can we go home now?" Nat pleaded, startling Shane out of his melancholic reverie.

Kelly glanced at Shane, her brow squeezed with sadness. Her blue eyes were wide with concern and her skin was pale with shock.

"No, sweetie. We have to go into town," she said, a tremble in her voice. She used a finger to push the hair out of Nat's face, and Shane remembered doing the same for his aunt less than an hour ago.

"But won't Mommy and Daddy be mad if we come home late?" Nat sounded oblivious to the fact that her parents were gone, though she'd watched them die. Perhaps her brain forced her to forget as some sort of defense mechanism. Shane was heartbroken for the girl but also jealous of her amnesia. "They yelled at you when you came home late last time."

"It's okay this time, Nat," Kelly said. She sniffled and cleared her throat, quashing some of her emotion and maintaining her role as big sister. "Mommy and Daddy want us to take a field trip with Shane."

"A field trip." Nat brightened a little. "Are we going to the zoo?"

"Maybe. But for now, I want you to lie down and rest." Kelly patted her thigh. "You can't have much fun if you're a sleepy, grumpy bug."

Nat stretched out on the seat and put her head on Kelly's lap. "I hope Mommy and Daddy don't miss us too much while we're gone. Maybe we should call them later."

"That sounds like a good idea, Nat." Kelly's voice was weak and shaky like she might burst into sobs, but she kept it together.

The exchange filled Shane with pity, and he gained even more respect for Kelly. Because of short chats he'd had with her at church and school, which usually left him feeling like a peasant talking to a princess, he knew there was more to Kelly than her looks. But the attractive blonde cheerleader was stronger than he'd ever imagined. Shane pulled his shoulders back, shrugging off some of the despair. Her sense of duty caused him to cling to his purpose—keeping Kelly and her sister safe. It was the only thing that could save him. The blessed distraction seemed to help blood flow in his veins again and made it easier to breathe.

Petting Nat's head, Kelly hummed a lullaby. She sniffled again, and Shane leaned over and opened the glove compartment, pulling out a small box of tissues. Giving him a grateful look, Kelly took one and wiped her eyes, and then continued to hum to her little sister. A mournful undertone in her sweet hymn tore at his chest. It reminded him of when he had fallen asleep on his aunt's lap at the hospital, that night when his mom passed. She had petted his hair and hummed to him much like Kelly was to her sister. He was thirteen then, and was certain his mother wouldn't die. Shane had prayed so much that he just knew there was no way God would take her. But he did. And now all this.

"What happened back there?" Kelly asked in a hushed voice after Nat fell asleep.

"The dogs… they did what the cows did," Shane replied, not having the stomach to get too descriptive. "The odd thing is that they didn't attack me, even when I kicked them away. The same thing happened with the bees and my aunt. I was with her the entire time, but I didn't get stung once."

"Bees?" Kelly asked nervously.

"Yeah," he replied with a faltering voice, surprised he could even talk about it. "And hornets, wasps, yellow jackets, and everything else with wings and a stinger. There must've been millions of them."

"I'm sorry, Shane," Kelly whispered.

"Me too." He glanced at her. "I mean, about your folks."

They rode in stunned silence. Shane navigated the Ranger around cars entangled with farm animals and with other cars, the drivers all massacred in their seats or trampled on the asphalt just outside their vehicles. Kelly attempted to find answers to what was happening by searching the internet with her smart phone. She couldn't keep a signal long enough to complete a web search, but didn't stop trying after most people would've given up. Shane sensed she was using it as an excuse not to look out the windshield at the carnage they encountered every few minutes. She finally gave up and tried to call her friends, her eyes focused on Nat in her lap. Her phone continuously rang or she'd get a busy signal. As with Shane's earlier efforts, no one answered.

"This thing is useless," Kelly said after a half hour, shoving it into her pocket.

"Maybe all this weird weather is messing with the reception." Shane squinted at another bright flash of lightning. It fractured the darkness with its blinding jaggedness, illuminating a tractor in the middle of a field to his left. In the split second the world was lit up, he saw a man slumped in the seat. Shane's stomach twisted. The farmer was dead. He'd seen lots of death, but somehow the tractor alone in the field with the man dangling over the steering wheel seemed to hit harder than the last few he'd encountered on the road.

"The cows didn't go after Nat and me either," Kelly mused. "It's like the animals only want to kill the adults."

"Somebody out there has to know what's going on," he whispered, reaching down and clicking on the old radio.

The Christian station Granny usually listened to came on, a prerecorded program about a drug addict who was born again playing. The numbness caused by all the death Shane had seen retreated at the sound of another person's voice. His heart raced and perspiration beaded on his face. He needed to know what was happening, what made the animals and insects go mad, but he also feared the answer. The little boy in him wanted to go home and crawl into bed, where he would pull the sheets over his head and wait until all this passed. The young man in Shane knew hiding wouldn't resolve anything. He had to face whatever evil was out there, causing the creatures to kill. Searching for news, he turned the dial up through the stations.

He stopped at his favorite alternative radio station. The static faded, so he knew the dial was in the right place, but only eerie silence came from the old radio's speakers. Turning the dial higher, he passed the country channel his dad liked—still nothing. No one seemed to be manning the stations. After going to the top of the dial, he clicked over to AM and began rolling back down.

"It's like everyone in the world is gone," Kelly whispered.

"Well, we're not," Shane corrected, a firmness in his voice he didn't expect. "And that means it's likely more people are still alive." He was trying to convince himself as much as her.

What if they were the last people alive on the planet?

"I hope you're right." Kelly's voice faltered, like she might start crying again.

"I know I am." Shane reached over and put a hand on her shoulder. "Don't worry. When we get to town, we'll find lots of other people. Just you wait and see."

His words made him ill. They sounded too much like the promises he'd made to his aunt when he tried to get her to the hospital, right before she died. Truth be told, Shane didn't know if anyone else had survived. And he feared it might just be a matter of time before the animals and insects turned on him, Kelly, and Nat. He never felt so lost and out of control.

Wanting to subdue the sense of helplessness, he made

a plan to go to the hardware store and get some guns. He'd stock up on bug spray as well so they'd have a chance if the hornets attacked again. One thing was for certain, he was done with seeing people get killed. He'd die before he let any harm come to Kelly and Nat.

CHAPTER SEVEN

A pileup of cars and an overturned cement truck, its lumpy cargo hardening across the road, blocked the west end of Main Street. Shane took the pickup around the lower side of town. The sun had been down for about twenty minutes, and the yellow streetlamps came on, but dreary darkness shrouded all the stores, no one around to turn on their lights. At this time on most summer nights, the restaurants and shops of the hilltop town of Leeville were busy, catering to a handful of locals and hundreds of tourists up from Atlanta to find reprieve from the smoggy heat in the cooler, clean mountain air. But now it looked vacant, so desolate and quiet it creeped Shane out.

It would be bad enough to think the inhabitants of the quaint mountaintop community had vacated due to some unknown event, rendering it a ghost town. Trapped in this nightmare he couldn't wake up from, Shane couldn't help concluding the silence was most likely because everyone was dead, all executed in the worst ways imaginable—their throats ripped out or their skulls caved in by beloved pets and livestock, or perhaps worse, killed by the venom of snakes and murderous insects.

Turning off the steep alley leading down to the road behind town, he drove past the body of an old man with a deer's antler protruding from his chest and glanced over at Nat. Thank goodness she was still asleep. He expected the town might be filled with dead and couldn't bear the idea of the little girl seeing it or of trying to explain to her what happened.

"So wrong," Kelly remarked, tilting her head down and shielding her eyes.

The headlights of the truck illuminated another victim lying in a glistening pool of blood up ahead. Three raccoons leapt off the corpse and waddled into the bushes in front of a bank on the left side of the road. The person's face and arms were ripped up, with clothing so bloody and tattered that Shane couldn't tell if it was a woman or a man. Looking at the mutilated body made him worry his dad might not be alive. Guilt surged in him when he realized he hadn't worried about him sooner. Had they grown so far apart that he didn't even care if his father had been killed? A bolt of pain shot through Shane's heart, and he knew the answer was no. He loved his dad, at least when he was sober.

"They're all grown-ups," Kelly whispered.

"Maybe the animals are only going after them," Shane replied. He made a conscious effort not to focus on any more of the carcasses.

"Look," Kelly exclaimed, pointing out of her window at four kids huddled on the loading dock behind the Piggly

Wiggly grocery store.

With all the dead around, seeing the kids alive was akin to finding water in a desert. He steered the truck off the street and into the parking lot. Before his mom died and his dad started drinking heavily, he used to bring his radio-controlled cars here in evenings with his dad and play until well after the streetlamps went on. His dad would tirelessly help him tweak the cars' little, gas-powered motors to get the most out of them.

The headlamps of the truck illuminated three boys and a girl. They backed into the shadow between the dumpster and the building. The relief of seeing someone else alive distracted him from the bittersweet memory of the time he'd spent in this parking lot with his dad. Shane leapt out and raised his hands.

"Hey, guys. Y'all okay?"

They didn't answer and huddled deeper into the shadows, seeming worried Shane had hostile intentions. He guessed their ages to be between seven and ten, probably all elementary or middle school kids. Their wide eyes and pale skin spoke to all the death they'd seen. Maybe they'd even watched their parents get killed.

"We ain't going to hurt you," he said gently, stepping closer to the concrete loading dock. "We're just wondering what happened here?"

"It was them bears," the shortest said, stepping forward. The streetlamp revealed a boy with disheveled blond hair wearing pajamas with bulldozers on them. "They came in the store and killed my mom and dad." He looked down at Shane hopefully, as if expecting he might be able to fix everything.

"Mine too," the girl with brown pigtails and wet, green eyes said, and then glanced behind her at the back of the grocery store. The other two boys nodded as if to say the same happened to them.

Wishing he had some comforting words, Shane stared up at the kids. What could be done? They couldn't be left here to fend for themselves, though he wasn't sure they'd be much better off if they came with him.

"No sense in you guys hanging out here." He put on his best adult voice, expecting it might calm them. "Why don't you come with us, and we'll try to sort this all out?"

They eyed him for a moment, and then looked at each other. The smallest pajama-clad boy who had spoken first gave a defeated shrug and climbed down off the loading dock with the others following one by one.

"What are your names?" Shane asked, hoping to ease some of their sorrow as he led them to the truck.

"I'm James," the smallest boy replied.

"My name is Sara," the girl said, a confidence uncommon for children her age apparent in her tone.

The other two boys didn't answer, glancing down at their feet solemnly. One pushed his hands into his pockets, and the other crossed his arms tightly over his chest as if to hug himself.

"They ain't said a word since we found them," James explained after a moment of quiet.

Shane looked at the two boys and smiled with all the kindness he could. "That's alright. I'm Shane, and that's Kelly in the cab."

At the back of the truck, Shane lowered the tailgate. With all the other unnerving crap he'd seen, he'd forgotten about his aunt. Her pale gray, swollen foot stuck out from under the blue tarp. Slamming the tailgate and spinning around, he blocked the kids' view.

"Why don't y'all go up and introduce yourselves to Kelly?"

James nodded and obeyed, the others following him around to the passenger side window. Kelly must've guessed Shane needed her to distract the kids. With that same warm, big sister attention she'd shown Nat earlier, she kept their attention by asking questions—how old they were, what grades they were in, and so on. Outgoing little James replied he was eight. Sara said she was seven. Shane felt the sudden weight of his and Kelly's new responsibility. Including Nat, they had five young kids to look after now, and he expected the number might continue to grow. But what could they do? Someone had to help these children. They wouldn't survive very long running around out here by themselves. He could only hope they'd find some adults soon, someone with some answers. But he was becoming more pessimistic with each dead body they encountered.

Satisfied Kelly had their focus, Shane reached into the bed of the truck and grabbed his aunt's ankles. Her flesh was cold and spongy in his hands, like it might slip off the bone. He swallowed hard and tugged her onto the tailgate. Wrapping the tarp tighter around her, he gritted his teeth to suppress a gag and then felt terribly disrespectful for it. Lifting her stiff body, he carried her over to the loading dock and laid her in the shadows. Succumbed by a wave of shame from his desire to get her corpse out of his arms as quick as possible, he kneeled and whispered a prayer.

The mournful words the energetic young pastor of their church spoke at his mom's and his grandmother's funerals were agonizingly vivid in his thoughts. Tears brimmed in his eyes and flowed down his checks. His simple prayer that his aunt made it safely to heaven, where she'd never suffer again and could rejoin her father, mother, and sister seemed insufficient. When he could think of nothing more to say, he stood and wiped his face with his sleeve. He told himself he didn't want to leave his aunt there in the open, but it seemed more important to worry about the living, and he didn't know what else to do with her. In his heart, he knew he just wanted to get as far away from her as he could. Her swollen body represented everything that was wrong, keeping death at the forefront of his thoughts and making him worry about his dad.

"I'm sorry to leave you here, Aunt Lillian," he whispered, looking skyward, "but you're in a better place now anyway, and you don't need this body anymore. Please forgive me."

A low, moaning growl carried though the backdoors of the Piggly Wiggly. It had to be the bears the kids mentioned. Having no interest in coming face-to-face with one of the vicious creatures, he spun away and jogged to the truck.

Kelly had kept the new kids distracted, and they didn't seem to notice him moving his aunt's body. Shane helped them climb in the bed, urged them to hang on, and then closed the tailgate. Getting behind the wheel, he let out a long, trembling sigh. He felt like he should be punished, like he'd committed a heinous crime against someone who'd always shown him nothing but sincere kindness and love.

"You did the right thing." Kelly reached over and put her soft hand on his forearm. "She'd understand." Her empathy showed in her moist, sapphire eyes.

"Thanks," he murmured.

Kelly's touch and her kind expression soothed him, but wasn't enough to erase his remorse. He started the engine on Granny's old truck, and with a last glance in the rearview mirror at the loading dock with his aunt on it, Shane drove out of the lot. He knew from experience, the pain of losing her would stay with him forever, eating away at his soul and tormenting him in the quiet hours of the night when everyone else was able to sleep.

"What now?" Kelly asked, her tone dismal.

"I reckon we should drive around town and see if anyone else survived. Maybe we can find some adults." He expected that wouldn't happen, but no other ideas came to him, and he didn't have the nerve to tell her he had no clue.

Turning right at the next intersection, Shane found a road that wasn't blocked and got the truck up onto Main Street. Buzzing streetlamps cast the five-block stretch lined with businesses in yellow light, so they could see the full extent of the devastation. Most of the stores' front windows lay in bloodstained shards on the sidewalk, and bodies littered the street. He navigated the truck around abandoned cars and did his best to avoid running over or even looking at the dead. Glancing in the rearview mirror, he wished he could keep his passengers from seeing the bodies. Their faces were ghostly white, their eyes wide as they surveyed the destruction. Shane knew the innocence and magic of childhood was ripped away from these children; they'd never be the same after this.

A handful of dogs milled about, sniffing trashcans and corpses with their heads hung low in that same rueful way in which the dogs that attacked Mrs. Morris behaved after they killed her. A horse stood inside Sanford's Pharmacy, looking out at the truck with a small, colorful box hanging from its mouth, pillaging the candy section. Shane knew most of the people who owned and worked in the stores on Main Street and went to school with many of their kids. He wanted to stop the truck and run inside the hundred-year-old brick and marble buildings to see if anyone survived, or maybe was injured and in need of help. But it was so quiet he knew he'd only find them all dead, mutilated by the animals and insects, and he didn't have the stomach see it.

The left side of the truck rocked up and then down, the tire rolling over something soft. Cold horror flowed through Shane. He'd just run over a body and feared it might be someone he knew, perhaps one of his friends' mom or dad.

"It was better down below, where there weren't so many lights," Kelly said, her skin losing color like she might be ill as well.

"Yeah, let's get out of here." Shane turned on Highway 72, the well-kept, two-lane road going out to the freeway.

They crept along, avoiding more wreckage on the

hill leading away from Main Street. It took fifteen minutes to drive two miles down to the high school. Shane worked on developing a new reflex to keep it together as he drove. The instant his eyes fell on a dead body, he shifted his focus away. He couldn't stand to see any more human carnage, and defensively made an effort to pretend they weren't even there. The particularly mangled bodies, or the random bloody parts lying in the road, he had greater trouble ignoring.

In the front yard of the church, a coyote darted out of the glow of the truck's headlights, a head dangling from its bloody jaws. The fleeting glimpse of this animal carrying away a piece of someone's mom or dad, or maybe the historical church's preacher, was enough to leave the image seared in his mind. Another scar he expected would stay with him forever.

A flicker of hope ignited in Shane when he saw the school. The parking lot had undamaged cars parked in it, and the lights were on in the gymnasium and cafeteria. His dad's mechanic shop was further down the road, near the freeway. Shane resisted the urge to drive to it. In all likelihood, his father wasn't at the shop. He could be at home, or maybe even here at the school.

"This looks promising," Shane said. He turned the truck into the school's driveway.

"Please, let there be people in there," Kelly whispered, glancing down at Nat resting on her lap.

CHAPTER EIGHT

Shane parked the truck in the fire lane next to the gym. He climbed out and gazed around the parking lot. He recognized several of the cars, including Aaron Morris' topless old Jeep. It hurt to look at the rust-colored vehicle. If Aaron were at the school, Shane would have to tell him what happened to his mother. He lowered the Ranger's tailgate, lifting James and Sara to the ground. The two older, silent boys climbed out and they all looked up at him as if waiting to be told what to do.

Kelly slid Nat out and held her cradled in her arms, the traumatized little girl never waking up in the process. Shane glanced around at the small entourage, their glum expressions as hard to endure as all the death he'd seen in the last few hours.

"Well, let's take a look inside," he said, walking toward the school with the others in tow.

The gym door squeaked when he opened it. Shane held his breath, eager to find adults who knew what was going on and would be able to take care of the children he'd picked up. If there were some alive here, then it could mean others had survived—his dad might still be alive. At least fifty kids of all ages mingling on the basketball court and sitting in the bleachers stopped talking and turned their faces toward him. Shane paused, scanning the room. Many of them had red eyes, and several had fresh tears on their cheeks. A wave of grumbles erupted across the gym, and the kids returned to their hushed conversations or lowered their faces back into their hands and continued to weep.

"They were probably hoping for an adult," Kelly observed. She'd slipped up beside him.

"Shane!" a familiar voice called.

Looking at the bleachers to the right, he saw Aaron climbing down. Shane walked over to meet him, the image of Aaron's mom being ripped up by the dogs fresh in his mind.

"Where are y'all coming from?" Aaron asked once they met him at the bottom.

"Granny's house," Shane replied. His insides quaked as he braced himself to deliver the bad news to his friend. Shane's eyes involuntarily shifted off Aaron's to the kids in the back of the gym.

"My mom was out that way. You didn't happen to see her, did ya?" He sounded so desperate and hopeful that it made Shane's chest ache.

"Naw," Shane replied. It came out before he had a chance to formulate the truthful answer. He felt like total crap for lying to his friend, but he couldn't bring himself to turn back now so he tried to change the subject. "What's going on here?"

"Nothing organized. I was here for practice when the animals went nuts." Aaron's lip quivered when he paused. "A bunch of coyotes came across the field and killed Coach Rice. We tried to kick them off, but there were just too many." He looked down at his shaking hands, and then shoved them in his pockets like he couldn't stand the sight of them. "The oddest thing was even when we attacked them, they didn't try to bite us."

"Seems like the same thing is happening everywhere," Shane said, sick from hearing about Coach's death. He thought of him almost like a father, probably because Coach was a million times cooler than his own dad was lately.

Nat woke up, and Kelly lowered her to the floor.

"Are we at the field trip yet?" Nat asked, rubbing her eyes with her little fists.

"Yeah, this is where it starts," Shane replied. He forced a smile, burdened by the notion that he was dishing another lie.

"I'm hungry." The little girl looked from Kelly to Shane with inquisitive, puppy eyes.

"We can fix that," Aaron said, tousling Nat's straight, blonde hair. "A few kids went to the cafeteria to make some food for everyone. Come on, I'll take you over."

Aaron led the way across the gym. Shane saw Joe Baker, Steve Thompson, Tracy Cyrus, and several other kids he went to school with. At least half of the people in the gym were younger, elementary school kids, who he figured must be the little brothers and sisters of his classmates.

They walked through the covered breezeway

connecting the gym to the rest of the school, and Shane saw Laura, the quiet Goth girl he sat next to in chemistry class. She sat alone in the shadows on one of the metal benches in the grassy area beside the sidewalk. Just enough light from the breezeway shown on her so he could see tears had smeared her excessive, black mascara down over her cheeks.

"You guys go ahead," he said to Kelly. "I'll catch up in a minute."

Kelly glanced over at Laura, and then back at Shane. No one seemed to like Laura at school—she ate lunch alone and drifted through the hallways like a silent ghost. He expected a look of disdain to cross Kelly's face, but she surprised him with a tender and understanding grin. Shane waited until the others entered the cafeteria, then walked over and sat down next to Laura.

"You alright?" he asked.

"No," she replied, fresh tears gushing.

Shane waited for her to say more. Instead, she turned and embraced him, crying into his shirt. He awkwardly petted her coal-black hair and let her weep. She had a floral smell, likely from her shampoo. It took Shane by surprise, not that he expected her to stink or anything, but she was always dressed in such dark clothes, and he'd never seen her smile. The flowery fragrance seemed to contrast sharply with her attire and personality. After a few minutes, she pulled away and slumped her head forward, putting her face in her hands.

Knowing she must have lost her parents, Shane wasn't sure he could say anything to comfort her. Under much less stressful circumstances, he'd tried to talk with her several times in class, to learn more about her. She was always ready with the kind of answers that ended a conversation quickly, or at least didn't offer any fuel to keep it going. Yet still, Laura's brown eyes seemed kind, and he expected under all that makeup was a shy girl who put on a front so she would be left alone.

"I'm going to go inside and get something to eat," he said. "You want to join me?"

Laura shook her head, not raising her eyes to meet his.

He stood and hesitated before walking back over to the breezeway. He turned and looked back at her, hoping she'd come inside. It couldn't be good for her to just sit out here and wallow in her sorrow. She didn't budge, so he headed toward the cafeteria.

"Shane." Laura's weak voice stopped him just before he walked inside.

"Yeah," he replied, pivoting on his heel.

"Thanks."

"No problem," he said, not sure what he'd done. He smiled as best he could.

Laura lowered her head, putting her face back in her hands.

Walking through the double doors into the lunchroom, Shane stopped and blinked to adjust his eyes to the bright fluorescent lights. Although thirty or so kids sat at different tables across the room, he'd never seen the cafeteria so quiet. Similar to the kids in the gym, they wore somber expressions, munching with disinterest on sandwiches and potato chips doled out by three kids working behind the stainless-steel counter.

"Shane," Kelly called, "over here."

She sat with her sister, the three little boys and the girl they'd picked up behind the grocery store, and Aaron, at an isolated table on the far left side of the room. He walked over, thinking he would've loved her to call to him from across the lunchroom under normal circumstances, in the middle of the school day. She might have smiled politely at him once or twice during lunch, but most days, she'd sit with the rest of the cheerleaders, engrossed in animated conversation. Shane would steal awed glances of her, like the rest of the boys in school, with no expectation that he'd ever have a chance to sit next to the blonde queen of cool.

"I got you a sandwich." She pointed at a plastic tray with food on it.

"Thanks, Kelly," he replied, slumping into the seat.

Across the table from Shane, Aaron stared with a blank expression down at his sandwich, probably worrying about his mom. The reminder that he'd lied about seeing Mrs. Morris stole away any joy he might've experienced from sitting next to Kelly.

"How's Laura?" Kelly asked with sincere concern in her voice.

"Pretty sad," he said, shocked she even knew the girl's name.

"Should I take her some food?" Kelly asked.

"Yeah, might be a good idea. But you should eat first."

Picking up his peanut butter and jelly on white bread,

Shane took a bite. He didn't have an appetite and gagged when he swallowed. Kids trickled into the cafeteria while they ate in silence. The lights made everyone look so pale, even more depressed. Shane kept hoping an adult would show up, that they hadn't all been killed. He forced down half the sandwich and drank his milk, then munched on the salty potato chips.

"Why do they call it peanut butter and jelly and not jelly and peanut butter?" Nat's sweet and curious voice broke the silence. She peeled her sandwich open and inspected its insides.

Everyone at the table looked at each other, weak smiles rising on Kelly and Aaron's faces.

"J comes before P, so shouldn't it be jelly and peanut butter?" Nat explained, sounding very serious.

"It should, shouldn't it?" Aaron said, peeling open his sandwich and looking at its contents with a thoughtful expression.

"Yeah, let's change it," Kelly added. "From now on it's a jelly and peanut butter sandwich and not peanut butter and jelly."

"Good," Nat replied. Seeming content that the world had been set right, she pushed the two pieces of bread back together and took a big bite.

CHAPTER NINE

"What should we do now?" Kelly asked after they returned to the gym.

The older kids used wrestling mats to make beds for the little ones, including Nat, on the other end of the basketball court, and the lights were turned down. Shane could tell that at least half of the younger kids were asleep, but could hear some of them whimpering, torn up over the loss of their parents. Several of the teenagers were moving from child to child, soothing them and trying to get them to rest.

Aaron and Kelly both looked at Shane, waiting for an answer. He couldn't imagine why they thought he'd have a clue as to what they should do, but he couldn't bring himself to say it. Their expressions demanded he take the lead, seeming fully confident he'd have the answers.

"Gather everyone together," Shane said tentatively, trying to formulate a plan. "We need to huddle up and figure out what to do."

Aaron and Kelly nodded, their worried expressions relaxing as if they were relieved to have an assignment. They herded the teenagers over to Shane. Almost everyone had the same need in their eyes that Kelly and Aaron did—they just wanted to be told everything would be all right. The burden of protecting Kelly, her sister, and the four kids they'd picked up behind the Piggly Wiggly was unnerving. Taking on the responsibility for all the kids in the gym felt overwhelming. When Shane asked for a huddle, he didn't expect they'd all end up staring at him, wanting him to give a speech. It quickly became obvious he had to say something, because no one else was going to start the meeting.

"Okay guys," he began with a shaky voice, trying to think of what Coach Rice would say. "We've all lost a lot today, and we're feeling like total crap right now. But we have to try to pull it together and make sure we're doing the right thing for those kids down there." He pointed toward the dark end of the gym, where the children slept. "They can't survive without us."

What he said sounded embarrassingly cliché to Shane, but a wave of agreeing nods and sounds passed through the small group of teens and they kept their eyes glued on him, their faces begging him to continue.

"Has anyone seen an adult alive since this started?" Shane asked to get some of the attention off himself.

They gave each other hopeful glances, but no one answered.

"Then we have to be the adults now." He looked around the group with his eyebrows raised, encouraging someone else to chime in. "We need to come up with some ideas. We need to make a plan."

"We could stay here and wait for someone to come for us," Aaron offered with uncertainty in his voice, glancing around like he expected an objection.

"Nobody is going to help us," Matt said drearily. Matt and Shane had been close friends in elementary school, but had grown apart over the last couple of years as Shane became more athletic and Matt brainier. "I checked the internet, and the same thing is happening all over the world. Animals are attacking adults and, in the cities, adults are killing each other. No one seems to know why."

"And there isn't much food left in the cafeteria. Soon, the electricity will go out if there is no one at the power plants to keep it going." This came from Billy, a nervous, short, red-haired sophomore who helped serve sandwiches in the cafeteria earlier. His family was one of the poorest in town, and he wore stained and outdated clothing that clearly came from donations or the Goodwill store. When they were in the first and second grade, Billy was the kid who always smelled like pee, and everyone used to call him *Willie Wee Wee*. He'd never been able to shake the reputation and was still one of the least popular kids in school.

"I saw this program on TV where they showed what would happen if all the people disappeared," Billy continued. "Things are gonna fall apart pretty quickly."

"What's gonna happen?" Shane asked, glad to have some other people giving input. He'd always thought that Billy was a nice enough guy and had made an effort to talk to him whenever he had a chance.

"Well, first the electricity will go out. Then nuclear

power plants and nuclear waste storage facilities will melt down, and it'll be like Chernobyl times a hundred, with nuclear waste spreading all over the place. Oh yeah, and chemical plants that use refrigeration to keep toxic chemicals in a liquid form will explode, and toxic gas will be blown everywhere." Billy's voice got pitched and panicky, his shoulders rising defensively and his head dropping like he wasn't accustomed to having people look at him, much less listen to him for more than a second. "And the animals that are used to people taking care of them will start killing each other. And the rotting corpses of those that died will cause disease. And—"

"Okay, okay." Shane cut the excited boy off. "I think we get the point. The world is going to go to hell in a hurry. So that brings us back to our problem—what should we do?"

"I think we should head south, toward Atlanta," Steve Thompson said, running his big hand over his short-cropped brown hair and then crossing his thick arms over his chest. He was a linebacker and the youngest player on the varsity football team. "There are a lot more people than animals in the city. There has to be some adults still alive down there."

"Yeah, but there are also a lot more chemical plants and rotting bodies. Which means more disease and poisonous gas leaks," Billy noted with a meek tone.

"Well, quit being a naysayer and think of something better," Steve replied, glaring at Billy with a look of disgust.

Billy took a step back and lowered his head, as if he wanted to disappear into the shadows.

"I think Steve is right," Tracy Cyrus announced firmly.

She was as tall as Shane was and had a short, blonde crew cut. Tracy never had a boyfriend, and rumor had it she liked girls, but she was so tough that no one dared to pick on her. "We should try to make it to Dobbins Air Force Base. My dad is on duty down there. The military will know what to do, and they can protect us." Being the commander of the JROTC program at the school, Tracy had poise and confidence that Shane respected and knew would be helpful.

"Okay," Shane replied, feeling a little less like the burden of leadership was all on his shoulders. "Those are some good ideas. Anyone got anything else?"

The kids glanced at each other for a moment, but none spoke up.

"Well then, I guess we have two options. We stay here and wait for help, or we head south and try to go to the military base." Shane asked the kids to raise their hands for a vote. Just over half wanted to head south.

"So it's settled." Steve sounded tired of all the talking. "What should we use for transportation? I don't think we want to be spread out in a bunch of different cars."

"School buses," Matt answered. "There are plenty parked out back. And I bet anything the keys are in the office." Being the shortest kid in the eleventh grade, Matt looked much younger than the others did. But having wrestled around with him a lot when they were little, Shane knew not to underestimate the nerdy boy who wore old school round-rimmed glasses.

"We should probably make sure they're fueled up, and maybe even put some extra fuel and water in tanks to carry along before the power goes out," Billy said. He'd slipped around the group so a few people were between him and Steve, but he still sounded on edge and gave a nervous glance toward the big guy when he spoke. "The pumps won't work without electricity, so it'll be hard to get gas. And the water will quickly stop flowing and become too contaminated to drink."

"I'm not going to be able to sleep tonight anyway, so I'll take one of the buses up to the gas station and get fuel," Shane said.

"I'll drive another bus," Aaron volunteered, looking a little excited about getting behind the wheel of such a large vehicle.

"How many do we need?" Kelly asked.

"Three should do it," answered Tracy decisively. "Two will carry everybody here, and we can load the third with extra fuel and food. The hardware store should have some jerry cans we can use for fuel and water. I'll drive the third one."

"You might want to grab all the weapons you see while you're there," Laura said, slipping out from behind the others like a dark ghost. "I wouldn't be surprised if we ran into some trouble down closer to Atlanta. If there are no police around to keep criminals in check, things could get crazy."

"Good idea," Shane said. "Thanks, Laura." Because of her quiet nature and the fact that she'd moved to town from the city just a year ago, Shane guessed most kids didn't realize she was one of the smartest kids in the school. He felt somewhat comforted knowing her brains were on their side.

"Kelly will come with me. Matt, you go with Tracy, and Steve, you help Aaron. We'll drive up to the hardware store and then get fuel." Shane scanned the kids' faces. They all seemed eager for an assignment. "Billy, go to the computer lab and search the internet to try and figure out what is going on. The rest of you gather all the food out of the cafeteria that doesn't need to be in a fridge. When we return, we'll load it into bus number three."

"Also, grab any blankets, jackets, first aid kits, and other supplies that might come in handy," Tracy added.

"Alright, let's make it happen," Steve said, clapping his hands like the team did when they broke huddle on the football field. The ritual felt awkward, and he got a few crinkled brow glances from the kids surrounding him, but then the group split up and everybody headed off to their assignments.

CHAPTER TEN

Using a fire extinguisher and more aggression than necessary, Steve broke out the window to the main office of the high school. Shane boosted Matt in and as predicted, the keys hung on the back of a closet door behind the principal's desk.

"There's at least twenty sets in here," Matt called out. "Which do I pick?"

"Grab the newest ones," Shane answered. "They should say Freightliner on them."

The school had purchased several new buses over the summer, and he knew choosing them would limit the chance of any mechanical problems.

Matt unlocked the office door from the inside and stepped out, dangling three sets of keys with numbered, red plastic labels hanging from them. He handed one to Shane, and Steve snatched another out of Matt's hand. Glaring at Steve, Matt gave the last key to Aaron. Tracy stuck her open hand out at Steve, staring at him impassively until he grumbled and surrendered his key to her.

They walked down the long, dark hall of the school

leading from the main office to the back parking lot. Their footsteps echoed off the high ceilings and the gray, metal lockers, and everyone seemed to be in sullen contemplation as they walked. Having not been used since the prior school year, the floor was waxed to a high sheen, and Shane could see his reflection in it, even with the limited light.

Pushing through the double doors at the end of the hallway, they got a view of the buses lined up in the back parking lot. He scanned the rows of yellow vehicles and spotted the shiny, new Freightliners on the far left side. Leading his friends to the modern, aerodynamic-looking school buses, he pushed the door in on the first one and climbed up its steps, settling into the cushy, green seat behind the wheel. Everyone else crowded in and leaned over him, eager to learn how to operate the big machines. Shane quickly showed them how to start the bus and explained all the controls and gauges.

"How the heck do you know all this?" Aaron asked, a bit of awe in his eyes as he gazed over the dashboard.

"My dad has a contract with the school to do all the maintenance on the buses. He taught me how to drive them when I worked at the shop over the summer. Luckily, they're automatics, so they're pretty easy." Shane's voice cracked as he spoke. He didn't know for sure his dad was dead, but the chances were slim he was still alive.

"Oh yeah," Aaron replied, his voice quiet like he sensed Shane's thoughts.

In the dim light from the security lamps at the back of the school, Shane could see Aaron's brow wrinkle. He reckoned he must be thinking about his own parents, and he felt like a total jerk for lying about his mother. He knew he'd have to remedy that soon—it wouldn't be right to keep the truth from his friend forever, but he had no idea how he'd muster the courage to tell him.

"Everybody cool with driving the buses?" Shane asked, clearing his throat and trying to keep his focus.

His friends nodded.

"I'll lead the way up to Main Street," he said. "We'd better hurry—it smells like it's about to rain." He looked up at the sky and couldn't see any stars or the moon, but at least the lightning had stopped for the moment.

Aaron, Tracy, Matt, and Steve filed out of the bus and climbed into theirs. Kelly settled in the seat behind Shane. The diesel engines roared to life one by one. Shane maneuvered his bus out of the parking lot, glancing in the mirrors to make sure everyone managed to get their buses rolling. He led the way up the hill on a narrow, tree-lined side road with fewer accidents on it than highway 72. They came out on the east end of Main Street, right next to what everyone in town called the hardware store but was more of a general supply store, carrying everything from animal feed and coveralls to toilets and hunting supplies. The front doors lay inside in a pile of broken glass, and merchandize littered the entry area. The two other buses pulled in next to Shane's, airbrakes hissing as they came to a rest.

"Looks like someone beat us here," Tracy observed, climbing out of her bus. She put her thumbs through the loopholes of her blue jeans and pulled them up, a look of determination crossing her face as she studied the building.

Shane had never seen her wear anything but blue jeans, an army green T-shirt, and paratrooper boots, except on the days when she wore her JROTC uniform.

"That means there's another group running around," Aaron added, scanning the area like he expected to spot them.

"Shouldn't we try to find them?" Kelly asked.

"I don't think so," Tracy replied, entering the dark building. "I think we should stick to our plan. At this point, we have enough people to worry about."

Tracy sounded a bit heartless, but her logic made sense. Thinking about the kids, sleeping back at the gym, whom they were already responsible for, stressed him out enough. The children in the gym, teenagers and youngsters, could only be a fraction of the kids in town. Worse, there were probably infants in cribs all across Leeville, screaming for their mothers and dying from thirst. What was Shane supposed to do, go door to door and gather all the children incapable of caring for themselves? And if he did, how would he tend to them? Nausea erupted in his gut, the anxiety stirred up by his concern making him ill.

"We'll go to the military base and then send help for everyone else," Shane answered his own questions with trembling resolve, looking at his friends for approval.

No one answered, apparently happy to let the burden of this decision rest on his shoulders. They stared at him for a long moment, their eyes wide with the trauma they'd experienced over the last few hours. They looked so young, hardly old enough to take care of themselves. As horrible as it was to ignore the other children stranded throughout town,

Shane knew his friends were already being pushed to the edge of breaking. They couldn't handle any more responsibility at the moment, and neither could he.

Matt grabbed a shopping cart and a flashlight from a rack near the front doors. Shane and the others followed suit, and they worked their way through the dark store, loading everything of any possible use into their carts. They found plenty of jerry cans for extra fuel and water, pouches of freeze-dried food that could be eaten in an emergency, and camping gear, though Shane hoped they would make it to the military base in a few hours and wouldn't need most of the stuff. He found pants and a T-shirt and finally got out of the Sunday clothes he'd been wearing since Granny's funeral that morning. He sighed with relief, slipping his tired and blistered feet into a pair of soft, padded hiking boots. His mood lifted when he stood.

Aaron made it to the back of the store first. "This is not good," he announced.

"What?" Tracy asked.

"All the guns are gone."

"No freaking way," Shane gasped, looking at the empty rack behind the counter. The glass doors the guns were usually locked behind lay in shards on the floor. The display case where the bullets were kept was busted open and cleaned out.

"Must have been whoever got here first," Aaron mused, sounding frustrated. "Greedy as all get out. They could've at least left us a rifle or two."

"They didn't touch the archery section," Kelly called

from the far right side of the gun counter.

Aaron perked up, and they all rushed through the ransacked gun area toward Kelly, like they worried someone else might run in and claim the weapons before they could get to them. The beams of their flashlights found a plethora of compound bows, crossbows, and arrows hanging on the wall and in empty whiskey barrels at the end of the aisles.

"I deer hunt with these," Aaron said, picking up an arrow with a triangular, black razorblade at its tip.

"Hey, it's better than nothing," Shane said.

"The good thing is, as long as we retrieve our arrows, we'll never run out of ammo," Tracy added, climbing onto the counter and taking a camouflaged crossbow with a scope mounted on it off the wall. Her eyes gleamed as she flipped it over in her hands. It had to be the most expensive weapon in that part of the store, the kind everyone would admire but few could afford. All the weapons in the corner had lethality in common. They looked badass, but Shane was nervous to think he might have to use one.

"Let's load 'em up." Shane grabbed an armful of bows and balanced them atop his piled-high cart, and then hung more over his shoulders. They felt foreign and uncomfortable in his hands. He was one of the few boys in town who never hunted, an embarrassing secret he hid from his friends. Hunting was a rite of passage in Leeville. It wasn't that he never had the opportunity—it was just he couldn't stand the idea of killing, so he'd always found an excuse not to go. The weapons and Tracy and Aaron's enthusiasm made him uncomfortable, but he relished the notion of facing down a bunch of wild dogs or charging cattle with his bare hands even less.

They made several trips in and out of the store, packing the third bus full. Tracy organized the supplies, shouting orders in an annoying and near condescending way the entire time. At least the work took Shane's mind off the horrors he'd seen that day. The jerry cans went in last, with Tracy using a black marker to label some for diesel and some for water. When they finished, sweat dripped off everyone's face and Shane's arms ached.

They took the buses across the street to the gas station and filled them up. The doors to the convenient store were unlocked and the lights were on. Shane entered, fearing he'd find the attendant dead behind the counter. To his relief, no one was inside. Shane retrieved some sports drinks for everyone from the cooler. Thinking about taking the school buses, cleaning out the hardware store, and now breaking into the gas station, he felt a sudden flash of shame. They were doing it to survive, and nobody was around to take money anyway, but all the same, it was thievery in a sense. The moment passed, and he almost laughed at his absurdness.

"We need to distribute the weapons between the buses evenly, so we can defend ourselves if we are attacked by the animals, or worse, people looking for a target," Tracy suggested. She lifted the last of the fueled-up jerry cans into the bus and accepted a sports drink from Shane.

"You should probably be in charge of that, and Aaron can help you find people who can shoot," Shane said, passing drinks out to everyone else. He picked up a bow and slung it over his shoulder, not sure if he'd be effective with it. Although he didn't like the idea of shooting at someone, he sure as heck wasn't going to allow anyone near him to be harmed. He'd seen enough of that.

"The bus drivers should have crossbows," Aaron said, handing one to Shane and taking his bow. "These babies can be left cocked and loaded so you can use them in a hurry if need be."

"How do you get a new arrow in it once it's been shot?" Shane asked, liking the simple point-and-shoot ability of the crossbow better, though he always thought of crossbows as outdated wooden weapons from the middle ages. This one however, had a carbon-fiber frame and a scope on it like a high-powered sniper rifle.

"They ain't called arrows," Aaron replied, demonstrating how to load one. "With crossbows, the projectiles are called bolts."

"Try not to sound like you're enjoying this so much," Kelly scoffed, dropping the end of a hose next to the water cans and walking back over to the spigot to turn it on.

"Hey, you have to admit—they are kinda sexy," Aaron called after her.

Shane felt a smile creep across his face. Everyone had been so depressed and down to business, it refreshed him to hear Aaron acting like his normal comedic self. For the first time, he felt like maybe they had a chance, that maybe they could all get through this if they stuck together and used their heads.

CHAPTER
ELEVEN

"Let's get this convoy back down to the school and try to get some rest," Tracy said in the slightly condescending way in which she always spoke. All the buses were fueled up, and the water cans were loaded. "It'll be easier to drive to Atlanta if we wait 'til the morning."

Although Shane suspected no one cared to have Tracy barking orders at them, everyone obeyed, climbing into the buses and looking too tired to respond. The diesels rumbled to life. They pulled out of the gas station one at a time, swerving around the body of a woman who lay dead in the street. Her neck was missing a huge chunk where her windpipe should be. Shivering at the thought of how bad it must've hurt to be killed that way, Shane wondered what kind of animal had attacked the poor woman. She wore a torn, flowery sundress and one shoe, and Shane guessed she'd lost the other one while being chased down by the animal like prey. He couldn't imagine a worse way to die.

Aaron put bolts on several more crossbows and stacked them on the front seats while Shane drove. This time,

Kelly rode with Steve in the other passenger bus, and Tracy and Matt took the supply bus. Shane realized he felt more depressed in Kelly's absence. By needing him, she'd pulled him out of the numbness that sunk in after his aunt died and gave him a reason to keep going. If Kelly hadn't come up the driveway asking for his help, he might've just lay down in the road and waited for death.

"Seems a little excessive, having so many loaded," Shane said, trying to distract himself from the numbness creeping back over him like kudzu swallowing a deserted building.

"It takes too long to reload these if they're needed," Aaron replied, grunting as he pulled the cable back on another crossbow. "This way you can fire off a lot of bolts quickly in a crisis."

"I think I'll leave the shooting to you," Shane replied, uncomfortable at the thought of seeing the bolt from one of the crossbows kill something or someone because he'd pulled the trigger.

"I'm not coming with you," Aaron said, sounding like he anticipated Shane would argue with him about his decision.

"What?" Shane looked at him in the rearview mirror.

"I have to try to find my mom." Aaron's voice trembled with uncertainty, and he didn't look up from his work.

Shane hated himself for lying to his friend. He'd known Aaron since they were little, long enough to recognize he sounded like he already knew his mom couldn't have survived. Shane deserved to be punched—he should've just told him the truth before. Tightening his grip on the steering wheel, Shane glanced in the rearview mirror at Aaron.

"She's dead," he blurted out, hating how insensitive he sounded.

"You don't know that," Aaron said, quiet anger rising in his voice. "She could be okay, or she could be hurt and might need my help."

Shane took a deep and shaky breath, and then let it out slowly. He twisted his hands on the big steering wheel and tried to organize his words. Aaron would've never lied to him, and he knew he owed his friend the truth.

"Earlier, when you asked me if I'd seen her," he paused and sighed. "I'm really sorry, but I didn't have the balls to tell you the truth."

"What the hell are you saying?" Aaron shouted, rising to his feet and leaning toward Shane, while still holding a freshly loaded crossbow in his hands.

"I'm so sorry, bro," Shane replied, feeling like he should be shot with one of the carbon-fiber bolts. "I saw her."

He waited for Aaron to slug him in the side of the head, almost wanting him to do it.

"Well?" Aaron's nostrils flared. Shane saw them do that before, when Aaron broke his arm on the football field last year, though the tall, blond running back hadn't shed a tear. "What happened to her?"

"Dogs," Shane replied, the word choking him. "I tried to throw them off, but there were too many."

"Damn you, Shane," Aaron yelled and punched the metal roof. He spun around and stomped to the back of the bus, sat down in one of the green seats, and put his face in his hands.

Seeing Aaron so upset made Shane feel like crap, and made the pain of losing his aunt and Granny resurface in full force. He leaned forward on the wheel, feeling like a dump truck full of rocks had just been unloaded on his head, bashing him to a pulp and suffocating him at the same time.

His thoughts drifted to his father. Shane couldn't be certain, but his dad had to have been killed as well. No one saw a single living adult since the animals went berserk. Wondering about how his dad died caused tears to well in his eyes. Had he suffered? He hoped not. He wiped the tears clear and tried to focus on the narrow road leading down to the high school, wishing his last moments with his dad hadn't been spent fighting.

Tall oak trees grew up on either side, their canopies connected above the road, blocking out the sky and creating an ominous, dark tunnel. Shane's bus coasted down the hill behind Tracy's, its transmission whining against the vehicle's weight. Steve and Kelly drove the last bus behind him. Shane wished Tracy would go faster; he couldn't wait to be near Kelly again. She sparked a little glimmer of hope in his chest, staving off the cold, dark depression settling in when she wasn't around.

Tracy's bus turned right at the bottom of the hill, and then roared and sped across the street before Shane could see the school. Dread knotted his stomach because he knew she wasn't the type to mess around. Hot adrenaline bursting through his veins, Shane pulled out of the oak tree tunnel and saw orange flames licking from the windows of the three long, red brick buildings housing the library and classrooms.

"Aaron," he yelled over his shoulder. "We got problems!"

Rushing to the front of the bus, Aaron leaned down and looked out the windshield. Shane floored the accelerator and zigzagged the bus across the street and into the dirt parking lot. Steve's bus slid up beside him in a cloud of dust. As soon as the diesels stopped rumbling, they could hear the shouts and screams of the kids in the school. They climbed out and converged in front of the buses.

"Look!" Matt said. "Those guys weren't here earlier."

He pointed at three teenage boys darting across the yard and into the side door of the gym.

"And they're wearing orange convict clothing," Tracy exclaimed. "Grab the weapons—they must be escapees from the juvenile prison."

Shane forgot all about the North Georgia Juvenile Rehabilitation Center, an experimental, high-security penal colony tucked away in the woods about five miles out of town. Rumor had it the center housed young rapists, murderers, and the nastiest of gangsters, not the kind of guys he wanted to tangle with.

"Come on, man," Aaron said, pushing a crossbow and quiver filled with bolts into Shane's hands. "We have to get in there and save those kids."

If Aaron was mad at him for withholding the information about his mother, Shane could no longer see it in his eyes. He ran toward the gym with the others. Kelly, Matt, and Tracy carried crossbows as well, and Tracy also wielded a large hunting knife in her free hand. Steve and Aaron, who

Shane knew hunted deer with bows every year, had high-end compound bows with quivers full of the razorblade-tipped arrows on their backs.

"We have the element of surprise," Tracy said. "They won't know what hit them."

"*No, no!*" A girl's scream came from inside the gym. "*Get off me!*"

Cackling laughter and hoots from several boys followed. Shane's imagination conjured up what horrible things the convicts might be doing in the gym, and any hesitation about attacking them vanished, replaced by boiling rage.

"Let's split up into two teams," Shane ordered. "Tracy, take Matt and Steve and wait by that side door. Kelly and Aaron, come with me."

"These boys will not negotiate," Tracy said. "We'll have to shoot first and ask questions later." The cliché warning made Shane's stomach turn, and he feared he wouldn't be able to kill once he was inside. His hands grew slick with sweat on the crossbow's handle.

"I got no problem with that," Aaron said, nocking an arrow and drawing the string back, the razorblade arrowhead aimed at the metal door of the gym. His eyes narrowed like he prepared to unload all his anger over his mother's death on the young convicts.

Once she had her team at the door about fifty feet down the side of the gym, Tracy glanced back at Shane as if she awaited his order. Another girl's agonized scream came from inside, making it hard for him to keep his rage in check. Knowing that being in control would help them stop the convicts, he took a deep breath and raised his hand, then dropped it to signal go like he'd seen the soldiers do in movies. He jerked the door open and rushed into the building with his crossbow leveled and ready to fire.

CHAPTER

TWELVE

The pandemonium inside the gym gave Shane's squad of rescuers an instant to assess the scene. Five boys dressed in orange jumpsuits had all the smaller kids corralled by the stage at one end. Shane saw one of the convicts slap James, the bold little boy in pajamas he had picked up behind the grocery store, on the face so hard it knocked him to the floor. The surrounding teen convicts laughed. He wanted to run to the child's aid but was distracted by thugs in orange lined up along the bleachers across the way. Their backs to him, they hooted and cheered as they watched something Shane couldn't see from his vantage. The bone-chilling screams and pleading of girls carrying from beyond the row of boys swept all hesitation and fear aside. He silently darted across the gym's polished oak floor on the balls of his feet, the butt of his crossbow rising to his shoulder.

"Hurry up, numb-nuts," one of the boys shouted. "It's my turn."

"Hold her still," another yelled.

At an angle between the convicts, Shane got a clear

view of the struggling girls pressed against the bottom row of bleachers. Rebecca Swanton, a proud redhead he'd gone to school with his entire life, pushed up for a moment and sank her fingernails into her attacker's face. The boy shrieked and hammered her back down with a punch.

Rebecca lay still, knocked out or dead, he couldn't tell. Murderous hate washed through Shane. He lined up the crosshairs in his scope below the asshole's bleeding face and tugged the trigger without a second thought. A subtle click and the crossbow's string thwacked. A quiet sound, yet it rang in his ears. The carbon-fiber bolt rocketed across the gym. Sinking into the boy's neck, its stainless-steel tip pierced through the other side. The kid dropped to the wood floor, blood spraying out over his hands, which he raised to cover his wound. His eyes wide with shock, he opened and closed his mouth—a fish out of water starved for oxygen.

"Get away from them, you bastards," Kelly shrieked.

The ferocity in her usually angelic voice startled Shane, breaking his dazed stare from the boy he'd just shot. Running at the thugs with her crossbow leveled, she shot one in the groin, and the boy dropped to the floor screaming.

In the time it took Shane to load another dart, Aaron and Steve launched arrows into eight more of the convicts. The uninjured boys backed away, releasing girls they'd pinned to the bottom row of bleachers. Steve shot again, then charged across the room and tackled two at once, smashing them against the wall. When they tried to get up, he slugged them with his cannonball-sized fists. The other juvenile delinquents tugged their orange jumpsuits back on and charged toward the doors.

"I'm going to kill every one of you bastards!" Aaron shouted and dropped two more of the escaped prisoners.

Shane, Aaron, and Kelly made it to the girls on the bleachers. Traumatized, they pulled their torn clothing over themselves and huddled defensively.

A loud boom echoed through the gym.

"Watch out!" Tracy shouted. "They have guns!"

"Aaron!" Shane yelled, spinning around and dropping to his knee with his crossbow raised.

"I'm on it," Aaron replied with lethal coolness.

Releasing one arrow after another, Aaron picked off the three boys who held guns. The others retreated out the doors, scooping up the guns dropped by the downed convicts. Shane, Aaron, and Tracy pursued the convicts out of the gym into the front parking lot. Sheets of rain came down, soaking them and making it hard to see. The orange-clad boys jumped into three pickup trucks and raced away, shooting at Shane and his friends. They couldn't aim, and only the red brick façade of the gym suffered any injury.

Aaron rushed into the parking lot and jumped into his old Jeep.

"Wait," Shane yelled, shielding his eyes from the rain.

"We gotta go after them," Aaron shouted. "We can't let them get away with that." He pointed at the gym.

"No, we have to stay together," Tracy warned. "Look what happened here when we left these kids alone last time."

After a long and defiant stare at her and Shane, Aaron conceded, yelling, "Arrgh," and punching the metal dash so hard that it should've broken his hand.

Lightning cracked and lit up the world, a deafening crash of thunder coming just after. The bolt touched down in the football field just below the parking lot, so close the air felt charged with electricity.

"Come on," Shane said, eyeing the sky with trepidation. "We need to load up and get the hell out of here. Those jerks will come back after they realize they have guns and all we have are bows and arrows."

"You've got a point," Matt agreed.

He stepped out of the gym behind them and stood under the awning covering the door, his empty crossbow dangling from his hand. His pale face and wide eyes expressed the shock of the conflict they'd survived—he looked like Shane felt.

The wind shifted and blew thick, black smoke from the burning parts of the school across the parking lot. Shane had forgotten about the fire, which still blazed in spite of the rain.

"We need to get everyone out of there before the flames spread to the gym," Tracy said, expressing Shane's concern.

Aaron slammed his fists on the dash and glared at the road the convicts disappeared down. Shaking his head with disappointment, he grabbed his bow from the passenger's seat and climbed out of the Jeep. His wet face contorted by hate and frustration, he stepped past Shane and Tracy, and they followed him into the gym.

The sounds of weeping victims made Shane want to

change his mind and go with Aaron after the convicts. The little kids were being tended to by Steve, who was surprisingly gentle despite his size and usual aggressiveness. Kelly and Laura worried over the group of assaulted girls, wrapping them in blankets and shushing them. Shane, Tracy, and Aaron walked toward Kelly, coming across a teen convict with an arrow protruding from his stomach. The convict groaned, his body curled around the injury.

"Please, help me," he begged, his face twisted with pain.

"I'll help you," Tracy said with loathsome sarcasm. She kicked him in the head with her black paratrooper boot, rendering him unconscious. Her hostility shocked Shane, though he didn't feel the least bit sorry for the scumbag.

"Keep your guard up," Aaron warned, slipping his bow over his shoulder. "There could be more of those losers hiding in the school."

"All the more reason we need to get these kids loaded and get moving," Shane replied, surveying the dead and dying lying in growing puddles of blood across the gym floor.

The adrenaline wore off, nausea filling its place. They'd killed at least half of the assailants, and though the escaped convicts deserved what they got, Shane despised seeing the one he'd shot. The attacker's scratched face looked younger and more innocent than when he was alive. His wide-open eyes already appeared dry and lusterless, his mouth frozen in its last struggle to gasp for air. Blood thickened into red stalactites hanging from the bolt Shane put through the boy's neck, and a large, green fly sampled some from the edge of the puncture wound. Had there been another way to rescue the girls without killing? He couldn't think of one, but it didn't make him feel any better. Trying to shift his attention to the living, he scanned the court and took a headcount of his people.

"Anyone seen Billy?" Shane looked around the gym again.

"He's dead," Laura said weakly, pointing to the shadowy space between the edge of the bleachers and the wall. His stomach knotting, Shane walked over and saw Billy laying facedown, blood spreading around him.

"He tried to fight off the convicts, and they shot him," Laura added. "He was so brave." She sounded guilty, and Shane guessed she must've hidden when the convicts came into the gym. Otherwise, they would've attacked her too.

"Kelly, can you and Laura get those girls loaded into a bus?" Shane asked, tearing his eyes away from Billy and swallowing the metallic pre-puke taste building in his mouth.

He abhorred how Billy was killed. It seemed sadly ironic the boy died trying to protect a bunch of girls who were never nice to him. After all the kindness the boy doled out over the years and all the crap he'd taken, he deserved a proper burial, didn't deserve to lay facedown in his blood and be left to rot in the dark corner where he was murdered. There was no time to dwell on it—Shane had to stay focused on the living now, and get them out of the gym before it caught fire or the convicts returned. Resolved to do something, he grabbed a blanket from the edge of the bleachers and gently pushed Billy over onto his back. Then, he said a quick prayer and covered the boy. If there was a heaven, someone as good as Billy was already there. The thought did little to quash Shane's anger and grief.

Kelly and Laura consoled the girls on the bleachers, wiping their tears and whispering to them.

"Get everyone loaded into the buses," Shane growled, rage threatening to take over.

"They need a minute, damn it," Laura snapped, glaring at him for his insensitivity.

"We don't have a minute," Shane replied, still sounding more aggressive than he intended. "We have to get going."

"It's okay," Kelly said, putting a hand on Laura's arm and flashing a warning glance at Shane. "We'll take them to the bathroom, help them wash up, and then we can load them on the bus."

Even with the chaos and his emotions pushing him around, Shane couldn't help but be impressed by Kelly's coolness and maturity, feeling guilty for his lack thereof. She was only a year older than him but seemed more with it than any adult he'd ever known—like she'd been through this a thousand times.

"Aaron, go with them and stand guard outside the bathroom door," Shane ordered, trying to adopt a smidgen of Kelly's self-control.

Tracy already ordered the rest of the kids in the gym on their feet, herding them to the far wall away from the dead convicts and out the back doors. Steve came over to where Shane stood, looking like he expected to be given a task. His knuckles were busted from hitting the criminals, but all the meanness was gone from his expression. His eyes were wide and a bit doleful, and Shane could tell he was also conflicted about the killing they'd just done. He guessed anyone who wasn't a natural-born, cold-blooded killer would feel like crap right now.

"Take a couple of boys and go grab all the food you can carry out of the cafeteria," Shane directed.

"I'm on it," Steve replied and ran toward the door.

"Steve," Shane called after him.

The big linebacker pivoted around and raised his brows. "Yeah?"

"You did a good thing in here," Shane said awkwardly, hoping to ease his friend's conscious. "We saved a lot of people."

Steve nodded and a slight, though painful grin rose on his plump face for an instant. "You too, man," he replied and then continued across the gym.

The downpour relented long enough for Shane to help Tracy get everyone outside and loaded up. Just after the last little boy climbed the steps into a bus, Kelly led the eight assaulted girls out. They looked glum and pale with shock, but only one of them still had tears in her eyes. Laura with her new crossbow and Aaron with his bow, an arrow nocked and ready, brought up the back of the line. Shane could see the adrenaline from the conflict hadn't worn off; his two armed classmates scanned the lot with wide-eyes, searching for threats.

"How are they doing?" Shane asked Laura once the girls climbed into the bus.

"Better," Laura replied. "Sorry I barked at you earlier, in the gym."

"No worries—I can take it." Shane gave a little smile. "Did those criminals do anything to you?" he asked, the question bringing his simmering anger to a boil.

"No. I hid when they came in," she said, casting her eyes down. "I wanted to stop them, but I didn't know what to do."

"It's okay." Shane put a hand on her shoulder. "You did the right thing. You couldn't have taken them on by yourself. You would've ended up like Billy."

"Maybe you're right, but I feel like total crap for standing by and letting those girls get attacked," Laura replied. "It won't happen again, that's for sure." She put a hand on the crossbow slung over her shoulder, a firm conviction rising in her expression. Shane gave his best effort at an encouraging smile, and she climbed onto the bus.

He remembered her crying in the breezeway just hours before. Now she appeared to have taken all her grief and turned it into steel. Everyone changed so much in a short time, seeming grown up, ready to fight and to survive. If he were told earlier today he and a few friends would fight off a gang of armed thugs and win, he would've laughed. Yet here they stood, on the other side of the battle, alive and safe—at least for the moment.

Chapter Thirteen

Pulling out of the dirt parking lot, Shane maneuvered his bus in behind Tracy's, and Steve brought up the rear in the supply bus. Violent cracks drowned out the sound of the engine, followed by a loud, extended hiss. The roof of a long classroom building collapsed, sparks swarming into the air and lighting the campus as bright as day. The brick wall with the school's mascot, an eight-foot-tall red devil with a pitchfork in one hand and a football in the other, still stood. Flames licked around the ominous demon, the flickering light bringing it alive. He always imagined the mascot inspired fear in their rivals, whose school buses had to pass it on their way in for football games. Seeing it standing tall, defying the school's collapse, inspired something warm in Shane.

The sparks settled and the flames died, having depleted the fuel. Shadows fell over the devil's mural, and it passed out of view as they turned the corner. The high school was such an integral part of Shane's life, where he hung out with his friends each day and spent evenings and weekends on the football field. To see it burned and crumbling piled more insult on injury—his hopes and dreams gone up in smoke, replaced by a dismal and uncertain future.

They left the orange light of the dwindling fire and made their way down Highway 72. This section of the road didn't have any streetlamps, forcing them to navigate around abandoned or crashed cars using only the headlights.

Shane turned the bus into the driveway of the lumberyard, following Tracy around a flipped-over RV. The lights fell on a cluster of mangled adults, all lying within a few feet of each other in a large mud puddle with the water stained red.

Kelly gasped, covering her mouth with her hand. She sat in the first row of seats, just behind Shane.

"They must've crowded together for protection," Shane said. Then he cringed at how calloused he sounded, like seeing the dead became as common to him as seeing the sun rise each day.

"Do you think we'll actually find some adults alive in the city?" Kelly's voice trembled, sounding as glum as he felt.

"I don't know. But if anyone survived, it would be the military."

The diesel grumbled as the bus climbed the steep hill leading to the freeway. His dad's auto shop was at the top, just before the on-ramp. Shane reckoned the chance his father had survived was remote. He knew he should just drive by and get on down the road. The buses leveled out after the long climb, and Shane grabbed the handset for the CB radio.

"I'm stopping at my dad's shop for a second," he said into the handset.

"Are you sure that's a good idea?" Aaron's concerned voice asked from the small speaker.

"No, but I have to," Shane replied without hesitation.

"Better make it quick." This came from Tracy, her tone scolding.

"I'll only be a minute," he replied curtly.

Shane knew she'd lost people too, but it didn't give her the right to act inconvenienced by him wanting to find out if his dad might have somehow survived. He bottled his irritation and pulled the bus into the parking area of the auto shop.

"Stay here," he said to Kelly, sounding as stoic as he could. "I'll just be a minute."

Kelly's blue eyes conveyed her uncertainty and concern. "Are you sure you don't want me to go with?"

"No—I'll be okay," he replied, giving her the most convincing glance he could muster.

Ignoring the expression saying she didn't believe he'd be okay if he found his father dead, he reached past her, grabbed a loaded crossbow from the front seat, and climbed off the bus. The solitary buzzing streetlamp bathed the shop and the parking area in soft, white light. It illuminated the stack of used tires on the left side of the glass garage doors, the row of cars with their hoods up in various stages of repair, and the fifty-gallon drums of motor oil sitting on either side of the entrance to the main office. A silent, soaking drizzle softened the light. Everything looked peaceful and normal on first glance.

"Where do you think he might be?" Aaron said,

causing Shane to jump. He'd slipped next to Shane without him noticing.

"The office," Shane replied soberly, pointing his crossbow in that direction.

He hadn't wanted Kelly to come along, because he didn't know how he'd react if he found his father dead. But he and Aaron were the closest of friends for so long that they were like brothers. Aaron knew everything about Shane—had seen him fall apart when his mother died and was frequently there when his dad got drunk and turned into a prickosaurus rex. Aaron's dad left him and his mom when he was a toddler, and over the years, he basically adopted Shane's dad. Though Shane was sometimes jealous because his dad was nice to Aaron even when he was drunk, Aaron deserved to be there as much as anyone, and it relieved him to have his friend by his side.

Aaron nocked an arrow, and they slipped between the parked cars toward the building. Shane saw an old, red Cadillac convertible he, Aaron, and Dad worked on over the summer. Dad promised they could have the car once they got it running. Shane felt a painful twinge and wanted everything to return to normal. Even if his father was a jerk half of the time, Shane wanted his old life back—wanted this nightmare to go away.

They hesitated at the office door. The streetlamp's light couldn't shine through the tinted glass, so they'd have to go inside. Shane looked at Aaron, whose eyes widened as if to say, *Don't expect me to go first.*

Taking a deep and shaky breath, Shane braced himself

for what horrors might lay inside. He grabbed the aluminum door handle and pulled it.

A thick, ammoniac smell wafted out to meet them. Shane's eyes watered. Quiet squeaking erupted from inside the office, accompanied by subtle scratching, like sand sprinkled onto paper. Shane stepped into the darkness, holding his crossbow ready like a SWAT team member entering a crime scene. Something crunched under his new hiking boots, and the floor felt wet and slippery. Shane reached for the light switch, and something tickled his fingers, causing him to recoil.

"Hit the lights," Aaron whispered.

His hand quivering, Shane reached out again, this time finding the switch. He flipped it up, and blinding light filled the room.

"Holy crap!"

They backed out of the office so fast that they almost fell on top of each other. The floors, walls, and ceilings moved, covered in millions of cockroaches scurrying in every direction to escape the light.

"What the heck was that?" Aaron asked, standing behind Shane, fifteen feet back from the office door.

"I don't know, but I got to go back in," Shane replied, a tremor in his voice. His skin crawled, and he wanted to run in the opposite direction.

Praying his dad wasn't in there, he crept to the office door. Most of the cockroaches found a place to hide, and only a few still rushed about. The office smelled damp and musty, and receipts pinned to the large corkboard on the wall opposite the door had holes chewed in them and were wet and covered with dark stains, probably bug waste.

At the right end of the room, a man sat slumped in the office chair behind the green, metal desk. Shane couldn't recognize him; his face was mostly eaten away. The cheekbones were picked clean, showing bright white under the fluorescent lights. But the blue Dickies the man wore were at once familiar. He spun out of the room, running into the parking lot. Passing Aaron, Shane dropped to his knees and vomited.

CHAPTER
FOURTEEN

"You alright, man?" Aaron asked with an unsteady voice, putting a hand on Shane's back.

"No," Shane cried. "I'm not alright! I'm sick of this. It's all bullshit."

He shrugged his shoulder, throwing Aaron's hand off. Sharp bits of gravel cut into his hands and knees, and he wept into his regurgitated peanut butter and jelly sandwich. His eyes clamped shut, and it felt like a belt tightened around his chest.

A delicate hand held a paper towel between him and the puke, wiping his nose and mouth.

"Come on, Shane." Kelly's soft voice cut through the agonizing haze of sadness crushing in on him. "Sit up for me."

She tugged him back so he sat on his calves, his head still drooping forward.

"We've got to get going," Tracy shouted sternly from her bus.

"Give him a minute, will ya?" Kelly retorted.

Kelly combed his hair back from his brow, her touch

soothing him like a dose of a powerful painkiller. "She is right though," she said. "Staying here isn't doing you any good."

"What's the point?" Shane muttered. "We got no one—they're all dead."

"You've got us, Shane," Kelly replied. "We need you."

"For what?" he whispered. "It's hopeless."

As depressed as he felt, he hated how he sounded so pathetic and wished he hadn't said that to Kelly. Shane already knew his dad must be dead, expected it before he ever stopped at the auto shop. But still, seeing Dad's corpse, sitting there in the office where Shane had so many memories—it felt like he'd been shot with one of the metal-tipped bolts from his crossbow.

Dropping to her knees next to him, Kelly tugged his chin over so he looked at her.

"You saved me, Shane. If you weren't there when my parents died, I don't know what I would've done." She pushed her hair behind her ear and studied him with moist, sympathetic eyes, forcing aside the darkness closing in on him.

"I need you. And those kids need you," she continued, pointing at the bus. "If you haven't noticed, everyone looks to you when they don't know what to do next. We won't make it without you."

Shane glanced at the bus. Kids pressed their faces against the windows, their wide and tearful eyes focused on him. Embarrassed at having so many people see him in this broken state, he looked at Kelly and tried to glean strength from her. He hated life, despised the world right then. But he couldn't help feeling a little flame of hope ignite in his heart when he looked at her freckled cheeks and nose, her soft, pink lips pulled tight with concern. He didn't care if he died right then and there, but he wanted her to be safe.

"You're right," he murmured dejectedly.

Kelly hooked her arm through his and helped him to his feet. His knees shaking, he walked to the bus and climbed on. After Shane sat in the driver seat, he looked down through the open door at Aaron, who wore a worried expression on his face.

"You okay to drive?" Aaron asked, his voice full of empathy but also caution.

"Yeah," Shane replied. "I'm fine."

Aaron studied him, uncertainty crinkling his brow. The dogs killed Aaron's mother, so what right did Shane have to give up when his friend was so determined to keep going? He cleared his throat.

"Really, man. I'm good."

"Alright," Aaron said, not sounding convinced. He gave Shane a concerned look for a few more seconds and then turned to walk away.

"Hey, Aaron." Shane stopped him.

"Yeah?"

"Thanks for going in there with me."

"No problem, man," Aaron replied. "I got your back—you got mine."

"I got your back—you got mine," Shane repeated. They said it to each other in the locker room before every game.

Flashbacks of a childhood gone forever—of casting their lines in the pond below the garage where they never caught any fish, playing football together from the time they learned to walk, and getting greasy up to their elbows learning how to rebuild car engines—rolled through Shane's thoughts. He watched Aaron walk to Tracy's bus and climb aboard. Rubbing his hand down his face in an attempt to strip away the mixture of debilitating emotions, he started the diesel and shifted the bus into drive. They drove out of the parking lot, and Shane didn't dare glance back at the auto shop, afraid he'd fall apart if he did.

His chest aching from his father's death, he steered his bus onto the on-ramp behind Tracy, and they entered the freeway. Heading south, they encountered only a few abandoned or wrecked cars on the road, so they managed to get up to a decent speed in spite of the thick, foggy drizzle limiting their visibility. At this rate, Shane reckoned they'd get to Atlanta in an hour and a half.

Every time he blinked, his dad's half-eaten corpse flashed in his mind, like the image had been tattooed on the insides of his eyelids. Kelly sat in the first seat behind him. He could feel her watching him, perhaps worried he'd lose it and crash the bus.

"How are the girls doing?" Shane asked, wanting to divert her attention. He felt ashamed about falling apart in the parking lot in front of his dad's shop, and the pity in her eyes wasn't helping.

"I'll go check," she replied.

Kelly stood and reached forward, putting her hand

on his arm. She gave it a comforting squeeze and smiled at him in the large rearview mirror. Shane tried to smile back. Then Kelly made her way down the center aisle of the bus, stopping at each seat to check on the passengers.

They had all the assaulted victims of the gym on their bus, as well as a few of the younger kids. Fortunately, there was enough room for each person to curl up on one of the green Naugahyde bench seats.

Shane glanced at the clock—two AM.

Every part of his body, toes to brains, suffered the bite of exhaustion, but he didn't expect he'd ever be able to sleep again. In the rearview mirror, he saw Kelly handing out blankets to their passengers. She paused at some seats and unfolded one of the green blankets over the sleeping passengers. He knew she had to be as torn up as he was, but she managed to put aside grief and be a caring nurse, offering her empathetic smiles as medicine.

"They're doing okay," Kelly reported after she made her way forward and returned to her seat. "Five of the girls have fallen asleep. The other three are staring out the window, but at least they aren't crying anymore. Rebecca's face looks pretty bad. I think she has some broken bones in her cheek."

"Hopefully, we can find a doctor at the Air Force base," Shane said. Thinking about how he'd seen the proud redhead get punched down, Shane was sick and angry about the incident all over again.

"Yeah—that would be good," Kelly replied. "At least she has some ice on it."

With what happened to the girls, Shane worried they

needed a doctor for a lot more than Rebecca's face.

"How's Natalie?"

"She's asleep too." Kelly yawned. "Has been since we left the school. Lucky her. I guess kids can sleep through anything."

"How about you? Why don't you get some rest?"

"No, I'm alright," she said. "Besides, you need company."

Only the growl of the diesel and the wind whistling over the bus disturbed the silence for a few miles. Shane glanced in the mirror at Kelly, who stared blankly out the windshield. Her drawn face and sad eyes made him worry she might be reliving the horror of watching her folks get killed. He wished he could take the memory from her and burn it, knowing she'd probably never again be the happy, carefree girl on whom he had a secret crush since middle school.

Funny how they hadn't really talked much before. Being a grade ahead of him and a year older, she'd always seemed out of his league. And every time she'd talked to him at church, he couldn't help but clam up. Now she looked to him for answers. Did she truly believe he could get her and her sister to safety?

Had she always thought so highly of him?

They traveled along a stretch of freeway with no accidents on it, and things almost looked normal for a minute. Then they were forced to slow down and steer around a motorcycle entangled with a buck. The rider lay thirty feet ahead of the bike, facedown. Shane guessed he'd been thrown over the handlebars when the deer hit him and died on impact.

"My gramps loved his Harley," Kelly said, sounding lost in memories.

Shane had seen the old man many times. He had to be at least six foot four, and he looked a bit like Abraham Lincoln minus the goatee. He'd always seemed so reserved and formal, wearing a suit to church every Sunday. Shane would've never guessed he liked to ride motorcycles.

"We sat in the backyard, by the pond, and had a picnic… just before it happened," she continued, staring out the window with a distant expression. "Natalie was trying to do a handstand. She had us all laughing so hard."

"At least you have that to hold on to," Shane replied, hoping to comfort her.

"What about you?" Kelly asked.

"My granny was buried this morning, and we attended a funeral service for her afterwards," Shane replied, unwilling to talk about his rotten last moments with his father.

"I'm sorry," Kelly said, sounding guilty for asking.

"No, it's okay," Shane replied, not intending to make her feel any worse. "I'm glad she passed before all this happened. The world was right when she died. And she passed away in her sleep."

"I suppose it was for the best," Kelly agreed. "At least you got to spend some time with your family before it happened."

"Yeah," Shane replied, wishing he and his dad could've spent the morning under the hood of a car together instead of fighting. In the shade of the garage, covered with grease, trying to diagnose an engine problem, they always got along best—those memories made Shane realize how much he loved his father, enough to forgive and forget all the arguments and drunken insults.

The red taillights on the bus in front of him lit up, startling Shane out of his sad reverie. Shane stepped on the brakes.

"The road is blocked up ahead," Tracy's voice chirped through the CB radio. "Looks like there's a bunch of kids hanging around a pretty nasty accident. We'd better stop and check it out before we get too close."

Chapter FIFTEEN

Shane brought his bus to a stop behind Tracy's, its air system letting out a loud hiss when he set the parking brake. Kelly handed Shane a crossbow, their fingers touching for a brief moment on the stalk. They paused, their gaze meeting above the weapon. Although sadness weighed heavy in her eyes, the right side of her soft lips turned up for an instant. A flash of heat surged through him, pushing back the numbing gloom. Before he could respond, she looked away and darted down the steps, joining Steve, Matt, and Laura, who climbed off the supply bus. The momentary thrill vanished, and depression enveloped Shane once again.

He was grateful no one said anything about what happened back at his dad's auto shop. At this point, no words could comfort him, and he feared he'd break down if they mentioned it. They silently walked forward together and stood next to Tracy and Aaron near the front of the lead bus.

"They look harmless enough to me," Aaron observed. He sighed with exhaustion and adjusted the compound bow slung over his shoulder.

"We have to be careful," Tracy warned. "It could be a trap."

"Don't be so freaking paranoid," Laura replied. "It's just a bunch of scared little kids. That looks like a church bus that's flipped over behind them."

"Yeah, well, there could be somebody hiding in the bushes off to the side, or behind that bus," Tracy retorted, "just waiting to ambush the poor fools who try to offer help."

"Seems unlikely," Shane said, trying to defuse the tension boiling between the two girls. "But we should be careful."

He guessed Laura and Tracy never spoke a word to each other until today—they mixed about as well as vinegar and baking soda.

"Look at them," Kelly said, sweet sympathy prevalent in her voice. "The oldest one can't be more than ten. And they've probably sat out here in the rain for hours."

"We should load them up and take them with us," Matt chimed in, his southern drawl thicker than anyone else's was. "The poor thangs—they must be scared half to death." Matt's accent hadn't been so strong a few years ago; his family was from Boston after all. Shane reckoned he was embarrassed by how smart he was and was trying to dumb himself down to fit in.

"I don't think that's such a good idea," Tracy persisted. "We already have a lot of kids to watch over. And what if the supplies run out?"

"Come on," Kelly scolded. "We'll be at the military base before morning. We can bring them with us and find someone to take care of them there."

"I say we leave them some food and blankets," Tracy said, acting like she didn't hear Kelly. "We can send help for them once we get to the base."

"You sound so insensitive," Laura scolded.

"We ain't leaving them here," Shane cut in. Shielding his eyes against the sprinkling rain with his hand, he glared at the arguing girls under it. "I'm going to talk to them."

Not waiting for a response, he walked toward the kids. There were about twenty of them, all of elementary school age. They squinted, blinded by the bright light from the bus' headlamps. Huddling closer together as he approached, they seemed to fear he'd raise his crossbow and fire at them.

"It's alright," Shane said in his gentlest voice, stopping fifteen feet away and slinging his crossbow behind him. "We mean you no harm."

He could see a few of them had tears on their cheeks, and they all wore ghostly expressions, like they'd been through hell. The warm August rain drenched their clothing.

Looking at the tallest boy in the group, Shane asked, "What happened here? Is everyone okay?"

The boy looked back at him, his face blank as if he didn't understand English. He had a scratch across his forehead, and a chubby kid next to him held a wadded shirt to his nose.

"It was the animals," a little girl who looked to be about seven piped up. "Horses ran in front of the bus and made us crash. Then rats killed Father Jacobs." She blinked at Shane with big, innocent, brown eyes, like she'd just told him she'd lost her favorite dolly and wanted him to help her find it.

"I'm sorry to hear that," Shane said softly. It sounded terribly insufficient. He shifted his weight, frustrated in an attempt come up with words to comfort the battered children.

"Y'all should come with us now."

"Where you going?" the outgoing little girl asked.

"Somewhere safe," Shane replied, walking forward and extending his hand to her.

"I wanna go home," she said, taking it and looking up at him. "I want my mama and daddy." Her voice broke, and tears puddled in her eyes.

"We're gonna get some help," Shane promised, his voice faltering. He looked around at the group of kids, trying to make eye contact with each of them in hopes he could offer a measure of reassurance.

Several nodded. Shane turned around and started walking back to the buses. He looked over his shoulder after a few steps and saw the kids rising to their feet and following him. Their heads hung low, and the rain plastered their hair and clothes so they looked like half-drowned kittens.

Tracy scowled, expressing her disapproval at taking on more passengers. Shane acted like he didn't notice, turning around at the front of the first bus and dividing the kids into two groups.

"Kelly, will you please help this group onto our bus?" he asked. "The rest will ride with you, Tracy."

He gave Tracy a firm look, expecting her to challenge him again. Surprisingly, she kept quiet and guided her group into her bus. Then Aaron and Steve stood guard as several of the passengers stepped into the trees alongside the freeway and relieved themselves.

"We should do a head count," Laura said. She held a crossbow, looking a bit like a petite comic book heroine with her jet-black hair and black shirt and pants. She had wiped her dark makeup off, rendering her face younger than usual. "It's getting hard to keep track of all these kids."

"Good call," Shane replied.

Laura turned and entered Tracy's bus, then came out after a couple of minutes and got on Shane's bus. He climbed into the driver seat, and she settled in the first row with Kelly.

"Seventy-eight in all," Laura reported.

"Wow, that's a lot of kids," Kelly mused.

The responsibility to ensure the kids' safety weighed heavy on Shane, making him wish Laura had kept the number to herself. Why did he feel liable for the kids in the first place? He hadn't volunteered to be anyone's leader—yet it seemed they forced him into the role. Shane couldn't wait to find some adults and be relieved of the burden.

"Let's just pray we get some help at the military base," he said. "Or else we're going to need a whole lot more supplies."

CHAPTER SIXTEEN

Shane watched Tracy ease her school bus filled with kids down into the median to get around the overturned church bus. When she turned it to drive back up on the highway, the tires spun in the wet grass, and the rear of the bus slid deeper into the ditch at the center of the median. She gunned it, and the diesel roared, but the tires sank in the mud. Shane put his bus in park and rushed out, waving his hands.

"Stop, you're gonna bury it worse," he yelled.

Tracy let off the accelerator and opened the folding door of her bus. "Too much damn weight," she growled. Her angry voice and crinkled brow made it clear she wasn't happy about Shane demanding they take on the extra kids. "Everyone off," she shouted.

The kids filed out in a hurry, seeming nervous that Tracy would snatch them up and throw them out by force if they didn't move fast enough. Once her bus was empty, she tried to drive out of the median again, but all she managed to do was throw mud twenty feet into the air and slide deeper into the wet muck.

"We'll have to tow it," Matt said. He and most of the dreary-faced kids had climbed out of the other buses to watch the spectacle.

"First let's get this wreck out of the way so we can pull her from the front," Shane said, eyeing the wreckage. "We'll have to push it with one of ours."

"I got it," Steve volunteered, rushing to the supply bus.

"Back into it, so you don't damage anything important," Aaron called after him.

Steve waved his hand in acknowledgment. With more zeal than necessary, he turned his bus around and backed into the rear of the church bus. The overturned bus screeched, throwing sparks when Steve pushed it across the asphalt. Shane worried they might attract some less-than-friendly guests with the ruckus, hoping they could get back on the road as quickly as possible. Once the church bus spun out of the way, Steve turned his bus around, and Shane and Matt rushed in and connected it to Tracy's with a thick chain they'd picked up at the hardware store.

"Ease it forward, Steve," Aaron said.

Either Steve didn't hear or his excitement got the best of him, because he gunned it and his bus lurched forward, causing the chain to go taut and bounce like a giant guitar string.

"Go easy, damn it," Shane yelled. Steve gave him a "oops" look, and he glared a warning in return. "Y'all need to get back," Shane told all the kids who stood watching the show, spreading his arms and herding them to a safer distance.

The chain creaked as Steve advanced. Tracy's bus

climbed up the muddy slope toward the road, and Shane felt certain they'd get it out of the ditch without a problem. The front tires made it onto the asphalt, and a loud popping sound like a shotgun going off startled Shane. Matt screamed. Shane spun around and saw him collapse.

The tense chain had broken loose from Steve's bumper and whipped across the road, clanging when it smacked against the side of Tracy's bus. After a stunned instant, Shane realized the chain had hit Matt. He ran over and saw the bloody mess that used to be Matt's left leg.

Matt wailed in agony, putting his hands over his injury, like he hoped to push the protruding bone fragments and ground meat back together. The flailing chain had hit his thigh, and only a narrow string of flesh seemed to be keeping the leg from falling completely off. Blood spurted from the wound, forming a puddle on the wet asphalt.

Shane cursed and fell to his knees next to Matt, wanting to help him. He didn't have a clue where to start.

"Now try to lie still," he said with a shaky voice, holding Matt's shoulders to steady him.

"Get some first aid kits, some blankets, and an arrow, Aaron," Tracy shouted, then squatted on the other side of Matt. "It's going to be okay," she promised, sounding like she'd seen this sort of injury a thousand times before. Shane knew she must be wrong—Matt had lost more blood than he thought could be in a person.

Tracy took off her canvas belt and tied it around what remained of the top of Matt's thigh. Aaron came running with the supplies, and Tracy took the arrow and shoved it under the belt.

"Twist this, Shane," she ordered, showing him how to turn the arrow to tighten the belt.

Squatting next to her, Shane took hold of the arrow and turned it. The metallic smell of Matt's blood and the warm sticky feel of it on his hands made Shane want to vomit, but he bit the inside of his cheek and kept turning the arrow around and around.

"It's got to be really tight to stop the bleeding," Tracy said. She sounded way too cool for the situation, but her calmness made Shane believe everything might be all right if he just did what she told him.

Matt stopped screaming, his eyes rolled back in his head, and he passed out.

"Wake up, Matt," Tracy yelled, slapping his face. "You have to stay awake."

Matt didn't respond. Shane tightened the tourniquet until it made the stub of Matt's thigh look like the tapered end of a sausage before the bleeding finally stopped. Tracy leaned down and put her ear to Matt's mouth.

"He's still breathing," she said, calm as ever. Opening the first aid kit, she grabbed a bottle of brownish-red antiseptic and poured it on Matt's wound.

"What the hell are we going to do about his leg?" Steve asked, hysterical. "It looks like it's been cut nearly clean off."

"There ain't nothing we can do," Tracy replied, sounding aggravated by the question. "The tourniquet has ruined any chance of saving it."

"We ain't gonna cut it off!" Steve stumbled back, his

damp face a greenish hue in the light from the bus' headlamps.

"We don't have a choice," Tracy replied, glaring at the six-foot-tall linebacker like it should be obvious. "Aaron, give me your hunting knife."

Aaron grabbed the handle of the knife hanging from his belt. He took a step back, looking at Tracy with wide, freaked-out eyes. Shane was dumbfounded, unable to say anything as he looked at his friends, his hands still holding the bloody arrow. Their voices sounded muffled and it was hard to breathe, like he was wearing a glass jar over his head.

"Give me the damn knife," Tracy ordered. "There's no other way. If we don't take his leg, he's going to get an infection and die."

"How the hell do you know?" Aaron shouted. "You ain't no doctor."

"Yeah? It don't take a genius to see it's gotta go. It's literally hanging on by a thread," she replied, holding her hand out for the knife. "And my mom was a vet, so I know a hell of a lot more than you. Now give it to me."

Shane didn't like the idea either, but it seemed pretty clear the leg was gone. "We'll take it with us, maybe they can reattach it at the hospital," he mumbled through a mouthful of bile.

With a horrified look on his pale face, Aaron stared at Shane. He tried to return his tall, skinny friend's sickened gaze with a resolute expression, unable to say anything else to support Tracy's dreadful plan. After a moment, a wild-eyed Aaron wiped the corner of his mouth and tugged his knife out of its sheath, handing it to Tracy.

She washed the blade with the antiseptic and held it above the wound. Shane stopped breathing and could tell everyone around him had done the same. Tracy inhaled sharply and exhaled slowly between pursed lips. She hesitated, glancing up at Shane. He discerned a smidgen of terror in her otherwise-stoic expression. Returning her attention to the wound, she lowered the blade and severed the small piece of meat still connecting Matt's leg to his thigh with one clean slice, like a butcher cleaving a cow into steaks.

Aaron turned and ran a few feet away, then spewed his last meal with loud and violent convulsions. Shane couldn't move, couldn't take his eyes off Matt's severed leg.

Aaron had slaughtered a lot of deer in his life, and Shane didn't expect him to get so ill. But then again, it didn't look like a deer leg lying there on the asphalt—it looked like Matt's leg, wrapped in bloody denim and wearing his left cowboy boot.

CHAPTER SEVENTEEN

Still green in the face, Steve helped Shane lift Matt off the wet highway and carry him to the bus. Matt was lighter than Shane expected, but then he realized a leg must weigh a lot and grew dizzy from the thought. Tracy followed behind them with the dismembered part under her arm, like she was carrying a rolled-up rug or something. Shane couldn't believe how calm she remained. He'd always thought her quiet and a little nerdy, never imagining this serious girl from school could turn out to be tougher than anyone he'd ever known.

"Lay him on the first seat," Tracy called after Shane and Steve once they climbed into the bus. "And keep him warm."

Shane and Steve carefully lowered the unconscious boy onto a blanket Kelly rolled out. Then she covered him with more blankets. Rushing down the steps and onto the freeway, Shane gasped for air and leaned back against the bus, trying not to pass out.

"You okay?" Tracy asked coolly, closing the lid on a long, blue cooler near the door of the supply bus.

"Yeah," Shane lied.

"Matt's leg is in here, on ice," she said, patting the cooler. "If we can get to the army base soon enough, maybe they can save it." She sounded skeptical.

"Good," he replied, wanting to quit talking about the damn leg.

He stared out into the dark forest, wishing he could run into the trees and find a quiet place to sit, a place where he could get away from everyone. He wanted to pretend none of this had happened, if only for a few minutes until his mind could clear.

Aaron stumbled out of the darkness, hunched over so much it made Shane taller than him for once. He wiped his mouth on his sleeve and looked at Shane with teary, bloodshot eyes.

"You're going to have to drive my bus," Tracy said to Aaron, her tone all business and no sympathy. "I'm riding with Shane to look after Matt."

Shane turned to Steve. He cleared his throat and tried to show a semblance of the calm confidence Tracy managed with such ease. "You should lead the way in the supply bus. It'll be better to keep our passengers in the rear in case we run into trouble."

After giving a feeble nod, Aaron staggered over and climbed into Tracy's bus. The rear tires were still fifteen feet into the median, but out of the deepest part. Looking like a zombie, Aaron leaned over the steering wheel and stared out of the windshield, his face slack with shock. He started the bus and shifted it in gear. The rear tires spun, spitting gravel and mud into the ditch, but the bus moved forward and climbed onto the asphalt. Even in his shocked state, Shane trusted Aaron was a better driver than Tracy was. Aaron had hung out at the mechanic shop since they were both little, and they'd raced go-carts on the North Georgia circuit until they were fourteen. Few kids in the school had as much time behind the wheel as Shane and Aaron did.

"Matt will be okay," Kelly announced. It sounded like she was trying to convince herself as much as anyone else. She climbed out of the bus holding new shirts and shorts from the hardware store and a gallon of water in her other hand. "He's sleeping now."

"Probably better if he's asleep," Shane replied, fearing Matt might be dying. "He'd be in a lot of pain if he were awake."

"Wash up with this," she held out the gallon of water, "and put these on." After setting the water and clothes on the bottom step, she turned and climbed back up into the bus.

Beyond caring that everyone might see him, Shane stripped off his blood-soaked clothing, down to his underwear, and rinsed with the water before passing the jug to Steve. The color returned to the big guy's face, but he still looked like death. After they got dressed in fresh clothes, Steve walked down the freeway with his head hung low and entered the supply bus.

Shane noticed the children who had exited the buses staring at him with horrified expressions on their faces. In the midst of all that had gone on, he'd forgotten about them. The numbness he'd experienced after his aunt's death set its teeth in again, and he stood taller. Images swirling in his head of his dead family and of Matt's blood squirting out of the hilt of his butchered leg blurred and then vanished, his mind becoming dark and empty. He remembered how much it frightened him when the blankness came after his aunt died. Now it felt like a cheap, wool blanket pulled around him, warm and almost comforting, but also scratchy enough to remind him it couldn't be right—that if he embraced the numbness long enough, he'd likely snap and go mad.

"Load up," he shouted at the gaping, young faces, annoyed how they looked at him like he had all the answers.

The kids blinked, as if waking from deep sleep. They focused on Shane for an instant longer, and then calmness flowed across their faces, his gruff instructions saving them from catatonia. Splitting into two groups, half marched over and climbed into Aaron's bus, and the rest walked past Shane, climbing onto his bus.

After the last kid was loaded, Shane climbed aboard and plopped in the driver's seat, ensuring his eyes didn't fall on Matt as he did. The metallic smell of blood permeated the air in the bus, sending another wave of bile into Shane's throat. When he turned the key, his Freightliner's diesel roared to life, the deep, soothing sound echoing off the dark pine forest lining the freeway. The smell of exhaust and the sounds, from a diesel or gas engine, had always been a comfort to him. Even though it reminded him his father was dead, he allowed the grumbling diesel to relax him once again. Steve's supply bus lurched forward, and he led the way, heading south. Shane pulled past Aaron's bus, taking up the second position in the small convoy.

"Maybe we should use this antibiotic ointment on the bandages before we put them on," he heard Kelly say.

He glanced up into the rearview mirror, getting a snapshot of his growing human cargo. The kids sat two in each seat, all wearing the same somber expression, looking like their youthful souls were sucked out of them and they'd never smile again. Tracy held a stack of gauze over Matt, with Kelly squeezing out little tubes of antibiotic ointment from the first aid kits onto them. Kelly's long hair was pulled up into a sloppy ponytail. Looking at her made a bit of the foggy numbness draw back. He had to get her to safety, if no one else. She was his focal point.

Further south, the road got more cluttered with wrecked cars. By the time they reached the exit leading into Canton, the buses slowed to a crawl. Steve used the supply bus like a bulldozer, pushing cars out of the way to clear a path through which they could drive. Shane kept his bus ten feet behind Steve's, so he couldn't see the road just in front of him. But the big vehicle rocked over something soft once in a while, giving him a sickening reminder that the dark road beneath his tires had the corpses of adults and animals strewn across it.

"How are you doing?" Kelly asked.

Shane jerked, having almost forgotten a busload of people sat behind him. Kelly slipped up next to him without him noticing, perched on the top of the steps, rubbing her eyes like she'd just woken up.

He opened his mouth to answer, but his parched throat couldn't make a sound. Kelly's brow rose in understanding.

She reached back under the first row of seats and pulled out a soda. Popping it open, she held it in front of him. Grateful, he latched onto the drink, draining half of it in three gulps. The carbonation soothed his throat, and the sugar and caffeine seemed to flow straight into his brain, waking him up.

"Thanks," he grunted, his nose tickling. "I'll live."

"Sun's coming up," Kelly mused with a hopeful tone, pointing out the open window on Shane's left side.

"Yeah it is," he replied and took another gulp of the cola.

She stood next to him in silence, slipping pieces of a granola bar into his mouth so he could keep his hands on the steering wheel. He didn't feel hungry and wouldn't have eaten if it weren't for Kelly. His last meal had been the meager jelly and peanut butter sandwich the night before, and he'd barfed most of that up, so he knew his stomach was empty.

"How's your little sister?" Shane asked, suddenly hating the silence.

"Asleep," Kelly replied. "She's doing better than I am." She fed him the next bite of his breakfast. "I think she's figured out that things aren't good. We had a long cry together, and then she started consoling me, telling me everything would be alright. I swear, it's like she's an old soul. So much wiser than me."

"I can see that about her." Shane twisted his head to the right and then left, trying to relieve the tension built up in his neck from driving all night.

The sky went from black to dark green. They crept across a tall bridge, and a loud screech of rubber sliding across the highway filled the hot and humid morning air as Steve pushed another car out of the way. Shane wondered absently how busted up the supply bus' front end was. He worried it might break down before they made it to the military base.

Kelly crumpled the empty granola bar wrapper and shoved it into her pocket. Sitting down on the top step, she leaned back against the partition separating the front right seat from the exit. Instead of the sky turning to a lighter blue with the rising sun, it became the unnerving lime green color it had been the day before, with ominous, thick clouds hanging low overhead.

"At least the wind is gone and the rain stopped," Shane said, looking up at the heavens and worrying about what weather might be in store for them today.

Three quarters of the way across the bridge, the supply bus in front of Shane came to a halt.

"There's another bunch of kids up ahead," Steve's tired voice chirped through the CB radio. "They look pretty rough."

CHAPTER
EIGHTEEN

Tracy stepped forward between Shane and Kelly, snatched the radio handset out of its cradle, and spoke into it. "We've got to drive by this time." She glanced at Shane, her steely eyes saying, *Don't be so dumb as to take on more passengers.*

After a long pause, Steve's agitated response came, "Well, what the hell do you want me to do?"

It was clear he wasn't taking orders from Tracy—he waited for Shane to decide. Shane's questioning gaze fell to Kelly.

"I think he's talking to you," she said, pointing at the radio.

Wondering why the hell he had to be the boss, he took the handset from Tracy and raised it to his mouth. "She's right," he said pensively. "We have to get some help for Matt." He released the talk button and put the handset back in its holder.

The sense he may have just condemned a bunch of innocent kids to death nurtured a thick lump in the back of his throat. But why? Did he really think the kids in these buses, who followed him blindly and looked to him at every crisis, were any better off than those out on the street?

The supply bus grumbled and rolled forward. Shane glanced down at Kelly. She returned a blank expression. Evidently, his answer to Steve wasn't so horrible, or she'd just go along with anything he said at this point.

"It doesn't look good down there," Steve's weary voice reported over the radio.

Steve steered his bus across to the right side of the road to get around a car flipped over onto its roof, and Shane could see what he was talking about. The bridge towered above the trees, allowing a clear view of the suburbs and city they drove toward. His thread of hope that Atlanta was unscathed vanished. Hundreds of bent columns of thick, black smoke climbed into the green clouds from every part of the city. Atlanta loomed ominous and crippled—a battlefield littered with destruction and rot, where in all likelihood the dead far outnumbered the living. It looked like Sherman had risen from his grave and marched through the grand old city once again, intent on burning everything to the ground.

"It's a war zone," Aaron's stunned voice came from the CB radio. Driving the passenger bus behind Shane, he hadn't spoken since Matt's injury.

"At least we don't have to drive far in," Tracy said. "The military base is just ahead."

A loud boom came from the south.

"I bet that's the army there," Tracy said, leaning over the front seat in excited anticipation and squinting her eyes as she looked through the windshield. "That's probably them fighting back."

"At least I don't see any animals around," Kelly commented. "Maybe they're winning."

At the lower end of the bridge, they drove past the kids Steve reported seeing from the top. The long line of boys and girls looked fresh from a holocaust, their faces and clothes grimy and covered in soot. Clean tracks striped their blackened cheeks from the constant flow of tears. Their heads hung solemn and low, most not seeming to notice the buses creeping by. A tall, skinny boy raised his gaze and contemplated Shane through the bus windshield. A massive, black bruise surrounded his eye and a trail of dried blood ran down his chin from a busted lip. The kid shook his head, as if to tell Shane to turn back, that they were going the wrong way.

"Why are they walking away from the city?" Shane asked no one in particular.

"They don't look like they're intentionally heading in any direction at all," Tracy answered. "I think they're just wandering."

Shane wasn't convinced. The line of kids resembled refugees he'd seen on the news, fleeing war-torn areas so far from Georgia that they never seemed real. His instincts screamed for him to turn the bus around and get as far away from Atlanta as possible.

"What if things are worse down here?" Kelly expressed his concern. "What if we run into more boys like those at the gym?"

"We got weapons," Tracy dismissed, seeming annoyed by Shane and Kelly's questions. She grabbed the CB radio handset and raised it to her mouth, "Take the next left, Steve."

The buses rolled past concrete barricades and signs warning they approached the entrance to the military base. Hope surged in Shane. Soon they'd be safe, protected by the military. Soon these kids would be out of his charge and someone else could worry about them.

"That's odd," Tracy said under her breath, her confidence faltering for the first time. "There should be a gate guard."

The red-and-white striped gate was in the vertical position, open and allowing them to enter the base. Not a living soul was in sight. Driving past, Shane peered into the guardhouse, fearing he'd see a soldier dead inside, ripped to shreds by animals or insects. It was empty. Another boom echoed across the runway in front of them loud enough to rattle the windows on the bus. Shane worried they might get hit by a stray mortar, but they'd come this far, and the sounds of fighting promised at least a few adults still lived.

Steve pulled his bus into a small lot beyond the gate, and Shane followed. Once they parked, Steve, Aaron, Shane, and Kelly climbed out and looked in the direction from which the boom came. Shane noticed the others carried their crossbows and compound bows out of the buses with them, and then realized he had his weapon in hand as well. He'd grabbed it automatically, without even thinking about it, and he reckoned he'd feel naked without it. How dramatically changed he was from the guy who woke up yesterday morning, who was nervous around guns and couldn't stand the idea of shooting anything.

"Something's going on beyond those trees," Aaron said, pointing at a thick grove of pines growing alongside the runway.

"Obviously," Tracy replied, condescending.

The distant rat-tat of gunfire came from the same direction.

"This area is certainly deserted," Steve said, using the scope of a crossbow to scan the base.

"Let's move the buses over to that hangar." Tracy pointed at a green, metal building a quarter of a mile down the road leading past the end of a runway. "It seems quiet enough. Then a few of us can sneak through those woods and see what all the noise is about."

"Or we could just load up and get out of here," Kelly suggested, stepping closer to Shane. "I'm not so sure we're any safer here than in Leeville."

"We didn't come all this way to leave without any answers, did we?" Tracy glanced from Kelly to Steve and Aaron, and then stopped with her stern and inquisitive eyes on Shane.

"Let's check it out," Shane agreed, deflated by the idea he was not to be relieved of his involuntary command any time soon.

He glanced at Kelly, hoping he hadn't offended her by siding with Tracy. She looked at him with trusting eyes, and gave a slight nod. For some reason, though he didn't particularly like it, they'd made him the leader. That being the case, he decided he'd do whatever it took to keep them from looking like the beaten-down kids they'd passed crossing the bridge.

"Maybe we can find more supplies here," Aaron said, walking toward his bus. "Maybe even some guns."

"Yeah, I'd feel a whole lot better with an M-16 instead of this dumb crossbow," Tracy said, slinging the weapon over her shoulder.

They climbed into their buses and drove down the road to the massive hangar at the other side of the runway. Tracy jumped out as soon as Shane brought his bus to a stop. With her crossbow aimed and ready, she slipped through a small, metal door hanging open before Shane had a chance to stop her. He respected her bravery but wanted to send Steve and Aaron in with her in case she ran into trouble. Moments later, the large hangar doors opened wide enough for the buses to drive inside, and Tracy stepped out and waved for them to enter. Shane drove his bus in behind Steve's. Inside the cavernous, metal building, the diesels' grumbles were amplified to a roar.

After killing his engine and setting the brake, Shane climbed out. Aaron and Steve shut down the other two buses, and they swept through the hanger ghostly quiet. It felt like they trespassed in a massive tomb.

"Anyone alive in here?" he asked, scanning the hanger. Translucent panels in the metal roof let daylight filter in, illuminating three fighter jets and an attack helicopter.

"Afraid not," Tracy replied.

"Do me a favor," he said, giving her his sternest look.

"Yeah?" Tracy spun on her heel and studied him with her stoic, gray eyes.

"Don't take off and run into any more buildings by yourself like that," he replied, trying to convey he didn't want to argue the point. "I know you're a badass, but we can't afford to lose you."

Tracy stared at him, as if formulating a retaliation. To Shane's surprise, she gave a slight grin and turned to investigate the hangar.

"Would you look at these babies?" Steve walked toward one of the fighter jets with wide eyes.

"It's odd that they're in here," Tracy said, sounding unimpressed. "Seems like they should be out, flying around and trying to protect people from the animals."

"Maybe the animals attacked the base, and the soldiers didn't have a chance to do anything but try and defend themselves," Shane replied, walking over by Steve and looking up at the fighter jet. On any other occasion, he would have been in awe of the vicious plane. But now, he was too worn out and depressed by all the death he'd seen to care.

"Well, there's only one way to find out," Aaron announced. "We have to sneak over and see what they're shooting at."

"I'll take that as you volunteering," Tracy said, climbing onto Shane's bus and coming out with an extra quiver of bolts for her crossbow.

"Everyone else should stay here and protect the kids." She pointed at the buses. "We don't want to leave them alone again after what happened at the gym."

"We have weapons now. What happened at the gym will never happen again," Laura said, a hint of defensiveness in her tone. She sat down on the bottom step of the bus and pulled her black hair into a ponytail. "What about Matt?"

"What about him?" Tracy replied nonchalantly. "I've done all I can—if he lives, he lives, and if not, that's just the reality of the shit we're in. Isn't it?"

Laura's jaw went slack, as if Tracy had slapped her across the face.

"Come on, Aaron," Tracy ordered. Not looking at Laura or giving her a chance to respond, she marched out of the hangar with her crossbow over her shoulder.

Aaron glanced from Laura to Shane, blinking from the shock of the harshness of Tracy's words. Shane nodded toward the door, too tired to worry about anybody's feelings getting hurt. He reckoned Tracy was more tore up inside than was obvious, that her tough girl act was a defense mechanism. Aaron shook his head with disbelief, like he'd never heard anyone act so rude. But then, without another word, he turned and trotted out onto the tarmac behind Tracy.

CHAPTER

NINETEEN

"That girl has issues," Kelly said after Tracy and Aaron had gone.

"I know, right?" Laura replied, standing up. "And you all thought I was the bitch."

"I'm not sure anyone ever thought that," Shane said, frowning at her. "If Tracy finds someone to help Matt, she'll obviously bring them back with her."

"I think we'll all have issues after this mess is over," Steve mused, hooking his big hand over the pointed nose of a fighter jet, as if to lay claim on it.

"Let's get these kids out and have them eat something," Shane said, knowing the idleness wasn't helping anything. "They look like a bunch of hopeless zombies sitting up in those buses."

Kelly and Laura walked back toward the children, and Shane added, "And give them something to do. Maybe they can scour this hangar for supplies and weapons."

He figured it might help some of the assaulted girls to have an assignment, something to take their minds off all they'd been through.

"Maybe we should move Matt out here too," Steve said. "There are some cots over by the wall. We could put him on one."

"It would probably be more comfortable for him," Shane agreed, fearing he might already be dead up on the front seat.

They moved a cot next to the bus and unfolded blankets on it. Shane couldn't shake the feeling they were creating a soft spot where Matt could lay until he went to meet his maker. Laura and Kelly led the other kids off the buses and split them into teams. They had the older ones search the hangar, and set the younger ones to organizing supplies. The kids seemed grateful for something to do, even chatting idly as they worked, and Shane hadn't seen most of them talk much since the incident at the gym.

Back on the bus, Steve and Shane pulled on each end of the blanket Matt lay on and lifted him like he was in a hammock. Matt groaned and opened his eyes. "What happened? Where am I?"

"It's okay, Matt," Shane replied, excited his old friend came around enough to speak. "We're someplace safe. We're going to get you off the bus now."

Matt cringed. "Why does my leg hurt so damn much?"

"It got busted up pretty bad when we pulled the bus out of the ditch," Steve replied, his look asking Shane if he should say more.

"But we bandaged you up real good," Shane added, shaking his head slightly to let Steve know he thought it would be best to leave it at that.

Pulling his end of the blanket toward the steps, Shane climbed down as slow as he could. Matt groaned in agony with every movement, but they managed to get the injured boy off the bus and lowered him onto the cot.

"My throat is so dry," Matt said, putting a hand to his neck. Shane took it as a good sign he could feel anything besides the injury to his leg.

"I'm glad to see you awake." Shane helped Matt take a sip of water. "You scared us pretty bad for a while there."

Matt's eyes rolled upward, his eyelids fluttering. The smidgen of color he had left in his cheeks faded, and he laid his head back on the rolled-up blanket they'd made for him to use as a pillow, panting like he just finished a marathon.

"Did we make it to the military base?"

"Yeah, we did," Shane replied, glancing around the hangar.

His face distorted with a wave of pain. When he recovered, he whispered, "Did you find out what the heck is going on?" He didn't open his eyes again.

"Not yet," Shane replied. "We haven't found any adults here either." After how upset Aaron got when Shane withheld the fact he'd seen his mother die, Shane couldn't totally lie to Matt. He would want to know the truth if they traded places.

"Oh, that sucks," Matt mumbled, demoralized.

His body stiffened, every muscle tightening. His eyelids squeezed together and his pallor became a grayish-green hue. With an agonized groan, he pushed up off the cot, and Shane grabbed both of the boy's arms. Before he could press him down, Matt surrendered and collapsed onto the cot. His breathing deepened and his face went slack, not peaceful, but at least no longer contorted with pain.

"Don't worry, man," Shane whispered, placing his hand on Matt's forehead. It felt hot and dry, a fever setting in. "We'll figure all this out and get you some help."

Matt didn't stir again. Memories of playing at his house when they were little flashed through Shane's mind. Matt had the biggest Lego collection Shane had ever saw, and they used to spend hours building massive cities with the blocks, only to gleefully knock them down, acting like giants attacking the plastic skyscrapers.

Saddened by the thought that those fun-filled afternoons were gone forever, Shane lifted the blanket covering the stub of Matt's leg, his reverie transforming into cold dread. Blood soaked through the gauze, all brown and red. Feeling sick and wishing he hadn't taken a look, Shane covered the wound. At least Matt still seemed to know what was going on around him; it had to be a good sign. But Shane feared he'd get a lot worse if they didn't find a doctor soon. He remembered a history class on the Civil War where the teacher said more than eighty percent of the soldiers who had a leg amputated died of infection. Matt's chances of survival diminished with each passing hour. At this point, he could only wait and hope Tracy and Aaron would return with good news.

Making his way across the hangar, Shane found the bathroom. Alone for a moment, he splashed cold water on his face and leaned on the sink, looking into the mirror.

Heavy, dark bags had swollen up under his bloodshot eyes, and his skin looked pale from exhaustion. He'd need to sleep soon, but after all the stuff he'd seen, he feared the nightmares awaiting him if he dared close his eyes.

A whirlwind of the last twenty-four hours of hell replayed in his mind as he stared at his reflection: his grandmother's wake, the fight with his dad, his aunt's death, and then Ms. Morris', the incident at the gym, his dad's roach-eaten corpse, and Matt's injury. Less than one day passed since the sky turned green and the animals went mad. It felt like a year. How much more could he take before he snapped? He wanted to crawl into a corner and hide until all this passed and things returned to normal. But things would never be normal again, even if they did find help.

"There you are." Steve's tired voice broke Shane away from the mirror. "Been look'n all over for you." He walked into the bathroom and leaned against the doorjamb. The skin under his eyes was swollen and discolored too, exhaustion's toll. "We found a military radio you should check out. It seems to be able to pick up everything the soldiers are saying."

Looking at his big friend, Shane realized he couldn't snap, regardless of how bad it got. For some unknown reason, these kids adopted him as their leader. He stared at Steve's downtrodden face, tempted to ask why they needed him to look at it. Couldn't they figure out what they should do on their own for once? Steve's brow raised, his expression saying, *You're the boss—tell us what to do.* Shane grabbed a paper towel, buried his face in it to dry off the dripping water, and sighed.

"Alright—let's have a look," Shane said, wadding up the paper towel and tossing it into the trash.

Relief crossed Steve's face. Perhaps he sensed Shane considered objecting to his role as the leader. He nodded and walked out of the bathroom with Shane on his heels.

CHAPTER TWENTY

In the main bay of the hangar, Laura supervised the little kids folding blankets, and Kelly had the older girls preparing food on three tables they found and set up next to the buses. Off to one side, the kids piled equipment and supplies they gathered from the hangar. One of the teenage girls and two boys from the overturned church bus who looked to be about twelve years old sat around a green box with an antenna rising from it and a black telephone receiver hanging from one side. Steve led Shane to them.

"Okay guys, we'll take it from here," Steve said.

The boys and the girl looked up at him as if to say, *It's ours; we found it.*

"Go get something to eat," Steve growled.

Spurred by the linebacker's gruff tone, they hopped to their feet and walked to the tables where the food was laid out. Steve lifted the radio and carried it over to a desk by the metal wall of the hangar.

"That thing looks kinda old," Shane commented.

"Yeah, but it was plugged in and charging when we

found it, and it works. We got a lot of static at first," Steve said, clicking the radio on. "Then we managed to pick up some soldiers talking back and forth to each other." He held the old telephone-style handset to his ear and adjusted the knobs on top of the radio. Then he passed the handset to Shane.

"...*roger that, I have enemy on my flank—request mortar support...*" a voice said.

"*They got our mortars, Captain,*" another man responded, sounding hysterical. "*They've busted through our parameter and are mowing us down.*" The popping sounds of gunfire, along with the screams of fighting and dying soldiers came through the speaker. "*We can't hold them—*" the voice cut off.

"*Peterson?*" the first man said. "*Peterson, do you read me?*"

After a distorted boom, the radio went silent. Steve looked at Shane with wide, questioning eyes.

"It doesn't sound good out there," Shane said, wondering who the soldiers were fighting. It didn't sound like they fought the animals, more like another army. "Let's try some more channels and see if we can learn anything useful."

"This could take a while," Steve replied, looking down at the radio and scratching his chin. "There must be nearly a thousand channels on this thing."

"Well, it ain't like we have a whole hell of a lot else we can do at the moment," Shane replied, patting Steve's shoulder. He unfolded a chair leaning against the wall and set it next to the table.

"Thanks," Steve said, lowering his stocky, six-foot-four-inch frame onto the chair with a tired grunt. Not wasting any time in getting to the task Shane gave him, Steve turned the dial on the radio and held the handset to his ear, then turned to the next channel and continued listening.

After waiting five minutes, anticipating Steve would find something else, Shane gave up and went over to the food tables. Under Kelly's direction, the girls sorted snack bars, chips, sodas, and other food they picked up at the hardware store and the gas station. They also made a stack of sandwiches from the food they'd gotten at the high school cafeteria and put out some military rations they found in the hangar. Shane picked up a soda and a granola bar, figuring he couldn't get anything else down. He walked over and sat on the bottom step of the bus nearest to Matt and cracked open the soda.

"Hey," Kelly said sweetly, squeezing in next to him.

"Hey," he replied, soothed by the warmth of her body touching his. "Good job with those kids."

"Thanks." Kelly stifled a yawn.

"How are you holding up?"

"I'm still alive."

"That's something," Shane replied, taking a small bite of the granola bar. "We'll all need to get some sleep soon."

"Yeah, I was just hoping Tracy and Aaron would return with good news first," Kelly said.

"Me too." Shane glanced at the door where they exited. "Maybe you should lie down though. I'll wake you when they get back."

"Maybe," Kelly said, then stood and walked to where

the little kids were playing. She scolded a couple of boys who argued over a fighter pilot's helmet someone found in the hangar. A weak smile formed on Shane's face. He was a bit jealous of the little ones—they seemed to be able to play and have fun no matter how bad things got.

Matt groaned and mumbled something Shane couldn't understand. He put his soda down and rushed to Matt's side.

"I'm going fishing, I don't care what you're doin'," Matt growled, his eyes wide open and fixed on Shane, though not seeming to really focus on him.

"You're at the military base, Matt," Shane said, worried. "Your leg got hurt, remember?"

"*No! No! No!*" Matt yelled. "I didn't make the mess, and I ain't cleaning it up!"

Matt tried to sit, and Shane held him down by the shoulders. Running over, Kelly grabbed Matt's good leg and helped restrain him. Matt yelled some curse words and then fell into incoherent babbling, all the while struggling to break free of Kelly and Shane's grip. As quick and sudden as the fit started, he stopped resisting and passed out.

"What do you suppose is wrong with him?" Shane asked.

"I don't know, but he's got an awful fever," Kelly replied, holding her hand on Matt's forehead. "Maybe we should get these blankets off him and try to cool him down."

Shane did as she suggested, and Kelly went to the bathroom and came back with a stack of wet paper towels. She laid them on Matt's forehead and pulled a small packet out of her pocket.

"This is some Tylenol I found in a first aid kit," she said. "My mom always gave it to me and Natalie when we got a fever."

"Should we wait until he wakes up again?" Shane asked, concerned Matt might choke.

"No, I think he needs it now," Kelly replied, her nurturing, blue eyes studying Matt with concern.

Shane lifted Matt's head and Kelly put the pills in his mouth, holding a bottle of water to his lips. He woke a little and sipped the water, washing the pills down. Feeling better that they'd done something to help him, Shane lowered Matt's head onto the cot.

"What now?" Shane asked, looking at Kelly.

"Now we wait," she replied, putting her hands on her hips. "And pray."

CHAPTER
TWENTY-ONE

So exhausted he feared he'd fall asleep on his feet if he didn't keep moving, Shane made his way to the metal door through which Tracy and Aaron exited. He refused to lie down until they returned safely, wishing he'd gone with Tracy instead of sending Aaron. But he recalled a game last year when he'd chosen not to pass to an open receiver and ran the ball into the in-zone himself. In spite of the points Shane earned making the play, Coach scolded him for rushing the ball and not using his team. A true leader was not afraid to have faith in his team, Coach said. Shane had to trust Aaron and Tracy would be safe, and he was better off here, protecting the kids.

Turning the knob on the door, he pushed it outward slightly. The wind whistled around the edges and jerked it out of his hand, slamming it against the outer wall with a loud boom. Dust and gravel whipped across the runway and pelted him. Surprised by the sudden change in weather, he shielded his eyes with his hand, reaching out and grabbing the handle of the door. Scanning the tarmac in front of the hangar, he didn't see any sign of Tracy or Aaron. The sky glowed an eerie green, worse than yesterday. Squinting to keep dirt out of his eyes, he used both hands to pull the door shut.

"Looks like a tornado is about to strike," Steve observed nervously. He'd come to help when the door flung open. "And this isn't exactly the ideal storm shelter."

"It looked the same yesterday afternoon, but I didn't see any sign that a twister had touched down on our way here," Shane dismissed. "Maybe it's got something to do with how the animals are acting."

"I hope you're right," Steve replied, sounding skeptical and looking back at the children gathered near the buses.

"Any luck with the radio?" Shane rubbed dirt out of his eyes.

"Not yet," Steve replied. "But I have a crap-load more channels to try."

He lumbered to his table and plopped in the metal chair in front of the radio, leaving Shane standing alone near the door. The wind howled, and the hangar creaked. Shane knew how easy a tornado could rip the sheet metal building to shreds. He scanned the hangar, trying to think of a safe place for the kids to take refuge. The best idea he could come up with was to have them crawl under the buses, though a big enough twister would toss the Freightliners around like plastic toys.

When Shane made it halfway across the hangar, walking toward the buses, the door flung open again, a loud bang echoing through the building. The wind blasted in, blowing the back of his shirt up onto his shoulders. He spun around, and saw Tracy step in with Aaron behind her, pulling the door shut.

"About time you guys made it back," Shane said, relief washing through him. "What did you see?"

Tracy gave a slight shake of her head and walked close to Shane, combing her spiky hair with her fingers. Her typical stoic expression was replaced by one of intoxicating horror and confusion.

"It ain't pretty out there," she whispered, clearly not wanting the rest of the kids in the hangar to hear. "The soldiers... they're attacking each other."

"What?" Shane tried to digest what she'd told him, the unusual fear in her eyes making him anxious.

"We hid in the woods and watched them," Tracy continued, her voice trembling. "Small groups of soldiers fought until one group was dead. Then the winning group would split up and turn on each other. They're wiping themselves out."

"It's like whatever happened to the animals to make them crazy is happening to the soldiers too," Aaron said, stepping next to Tracy. Sweat drenched both of their faces.

"And the weather isn't looking good either," Tracy added, panting between sentences. "We saw a big twister touch down a few miles away."

As if to prove her point, the wind howled around the hangar. Shane could almost sense the building swaying back and forth, threatening to collapse on their heads.

"Let's pull the buses side by side, so we can hide under them if a tornado strikes," Shane said.

Shane and Aaron drove two of the buses alongside the

one Matt's cot sat next to. The diesel engines could barely be heard over the roar of the storm. Driving so close he knocked the mirrors off, Shane set the brakes and crawled through the window into the adjacent bus. The large, metal hangar door banged against its track. He'd heard the unmistakable roaring before, when a tornado passed by Granny's house last year and ripped off all the siding on one side with surgical precision.

"Everyone under the buses," Shane yelled from the bottom step. He glanced up at the creaking, iron rafters with concern.

"What about Matt?" Kelly asked, herding the children.

"We'll get him," Steve replied, looking at Shane.

Steve set the radio down, which he'd been clutching under his arm like a football. They lifted Matt and lowered him to the floor. Using as much care as they could not to cause him further injury, they slid him on his blanket under the bus. Matt didn't make a sound and felt limp when they picked him up. Shane worried he was getting worse, but there wasn't anything else they could do to help him.

The violent bang of the hangar door against the building evoked a chorus of screams. Laura and Kelly hurried the kids under the buses, the howl of the storm growing louder. A twelve-foot-wide piece of the metal siding ripped away from the hangar with an earsplitting creak. Through the jagged opening, Shane caught a clear view of the swirling, black funnel approaching across the tarmac. Trash climbed into the air, lifted by the vortex like dry leaves floating in the wind. Hundreds of feet off the ground, a tractor-trailer made a turn around the hungry giant, and he realized some of those bits of spinning garbage were massive. Icicles of fear formed in his veins. They were all going to die. He spun and ran to their hopeless attempt at a storm shelter.

"Get under the bus," he yelled at Tracy, Aaron, and Steve.

Scrambling into action, they dropped to the ground and rolled under the Freightliners. Shane flipped the tables and tugged them against the side of the bus facing the storm. The wind pushed him to the smooth, concrete floor, and he crawled toward his friends.

An earsplitting clank startled him. Over his shoulder, he saw the twenty-foot-tall, forty-foot-wide main hangar door bust free and fly into the air like a floppy piece of newspaper whipped by the wind. Shane dove under the bus between the table and the front tire. Steve and Aaron grabbed his arms and pulled him in further.

The main hangar door crashed into the first bus so hard that it rocked up off its tires, but fell back down and continued to shelter them. Shane could see the kids screaming, their mouths open and their eyes wide with fear, but he couldn't hear them over the deafening sound of the twister. The storm moaned, an enraged monster hungry for blood. The metal building screeched as it was ripped apart; the funnel had to be almost on top of them. Shane looked at the older kids and tucked his head under his arms, then rose up and pointed at the screaming children. Kelly, Laura, Steve, Aaron, and Tracy, along with several of the other older girls, got the hint and crawled from child to child, helping them to duck their heads down and cover them with their arms for protection.

Another large chunk of the building tore loose and slammed into the buses. Glass rained down, and then the wind caught the shards and blew the pieces at Shane and the kids. His skin stung where they hit him, and it felt like he was being torn to shreds. He decided at that painful moment they couldn't survive—this storm would kill him and all the kids under his charge. Wasn't it better to die this way than have animals attack them or end up turning on each other like Tracy and Aaron said the soldiers had done? As horrible as the last twenty-four hours had been, he was shocked to find he wasn't ready to give up, not yet.

Gravel, sticks, and debris pelted him, and the roar grew louder. A hand slipped around his arm. He turned his head to the side and opened his eyes enough to see Kelly crawling closer with Natalie huddled beneath her. Reminded of those petrified bodies found buried in volcanic ash in Pompeii, Shane lay on his side and pulled them in, his back to the storm. Through all the pain of being sandblasted, he found distraction in the passing thought that at least he got to hold Kelly Douglas in his arms once before he died.

The tornado persisted, the buses rocking off their tires from its gust. When the twister finally passed and the buses settled, Shane couldn't believe it hadn't lifted the long, yellow vehicles into the air. A lightning storm followed, softball-size hail hammering the metal roofs of the buses to a deafening rhythm only the devil could enjoy. Shane lay there, relieved he wasn't being pummeled by flying gravel anymore.

By some miracle or curse, only time would tell which, the twister spared them. When lightning flashed and lit up the space under the vehicles, Shane saw Steve, Aaron, and the other older kids had formed a half circle around the younger kids, protecting them with their bodies like Shane protected Kelly and Nat. Although exhausted and battered by the storm, Shane felt fortunate to be surrounded by such compassionate and brave people. He couldn't imagine how terrible it would be to endure all this without them.

The hail let up after a half hour and turned to pattering rain. His ears ringing, Shane felt warm, pressed against Kelly. A corrosive mix of emotional and physical exhaustion eroded his awareness. Although he fought it, wanting to stay alert and watch out for his people, his eyes grew heavier until, finally, he surrendered to unconsciousness.

CHAPTER TWENTY-TWO

Opening his eyes, Shane searched the darkness. Where was he? It didn't take long to realize this wasn't his bed—he couldn't be at home. He lay on cold, hard concrete in a puddle of water. Confusion and disorientation caused a surge of panic to boil through him. And then he noticed he was curled around a warm body. Silky hair tickled his nose, smelling faintly of roses and lavender.

Kelly.

Every horrid detail from the last day flooded his mind, drowning the flash of joy he experienced from waking up next to the hottest girl in school and making him wish he'd stayed asleep forever. His left shoulder, hip, and leg ached from lying on the ground. Fortunately, someone had put a blanket over him to keep him warm in spite of his wet clothes. Wincing, he pushed himself up enough to look around. He could just make out shadowy lumps in front of him, the kids who had become his responsibility to protect still asleep under the three buses.

A flashlight illuminated the area beyond the front

bumpers. He rolled the blanket covering him with his right hand and slipped his left arm out from under Kelly's head, replacing it with the makeshift pillow. Brushing her hair back from her face, he adjusted her blanket to cover her and her sister better, hoping a pleasant dream might carry them away from this terrible reality for a few hours.

Crawling out from under the bus, Shane rose to his feet, stretching his battered and achy body. His back and neck stung from what felt like a hundred cuts where the flying glass and debris pelted him. Heavy, green clouds overhead started to glow with the approaching dawn, giving Shane enough light to see the hangar was blasted to pieces by the tornado. Only one corner, standing just taller than Shane, remained. A fighter jet lay smashed and upside down beyond the foundation of the hangar, and the other aircraft was nowhere to be seen.

He turned around and looked at the buses that miraculously sheltered them from the twister. By some awesome stroke of luck, the metal walls and main doors of the hangar fell at angles against the buses, making a lean-to shelter that must've protected them from the brunt of the storm.

Tracy and Steve huddled in front of Shane, next to the military radio, with Steve holding the handset between their ears so they could listen at the same time.

His leg tingling from being pressed against the cold concrete for too many hours, Shane limped over to his friends. Tracy glanced at him with a distraught expression. After a long minute, with Tracy and Steve listening to the handset and Shane wondering what the heck had them so enthralled, Steve looked up at Shane, saying, "You gotta hear this."

Tracy stood and rubbed her hands down her face, groaning.

"What's wrong with this world?" she asked, walking a few feet away and leaning her head back, as if looking for the answer in the overcast heavens.

Shane reached out to take the handset from Steve, the anticipation driving him mad.

"Hold on a second, so it starts at the beginning," Steve said, the handset still pressed to his ear.

After an excruciating moment of watching Tracy stomp back and forth and curse under her breath, Steve gave Shane the handset. He adjusted the channel to reduce the static coming through the earpiece, and then Shane could hear a woman's voice.

"...This is Dr. Sandra Gunderson, head laboratory biologist for the Department of Defense's Low Environmental Impact Global Weapons Research Facility. I have recorded this message in advance and against orders from General Mires in case of a weapon malfunction. If this message is being broadcast, the Low Frequency Limbic Manipulator Weapon has been activated and, as I feared, has caused the death of everyone in the laboratory, leaving no one to shut it down. Designed to be used against terrorist cells worldwide with minimal collateral damage to children and the environment, the weapon causes all multicellular organisms to target and terminate adult humans, and will cause adult humans to turn on each other in areas of higher population density."

Now Shane understood why Tracy was so upset. He couldn't accept what he'd just heard—the damn government had caused all this to happen. He gave Steve a look of disbelief. Steve nodded, his lips drawn tight in an angry frown.

"The weapon manipulates magnetic fields and uses extremely low frequency energy waves that will penetrate the diameter of the Earth, so it is possible the impact of this malfunction will be worldwide. Initially, the animals and insects will be triggered to attack adults, average age of eighteen and up. But due to prolonged exposure to the weapon, we believe every twenty-four to forty-eight hours younger and younger humans may be targeted. Because of the nature of the radiation being use by this weapon, we fear it may cause some disturbances to weather patterns as well."

"Some disturbances," Shane muttered, sick from listening to the woman's voice. "Ain't that the understatement of the century?"

A slamming door was audible and then the woman began speaking faster and with nervousness in her tone.

"The central broadcasting array's controls are located in a laboratory hidden beneath the Georgia Dome in Atlanta. Tunnel access to the control room is via an entrance in room B101 of the state capitol building. The laboratory will be locked down and protected by an automated security system, so the only way to turn off the Limbic Manipulator Weapon will be to disconnect the batteries contained in a bunker just beyond the entrance to the lab."

The woman paused, and Shane glanced at Tracy, who leaned over and put her hands on her knees, looking like she might vomit. He knew she wanted to join the military once she graduated high school and heard her talking about West Point more than once. Now she found out the government she wanted to work for was responsible for genocide—for killing the very people it was sworn to protect. Shane wished he could do or say something to make her feel better, but she was so stoic and cold most of the time he figured she'd just get angry if he attempted to comfort her.

The scientist continued, *"If you are hearing this message, it is likely that you are young. I'm sorry we've done this to you. We have been stupid and arrogant to play with such dangerous technology, which I fear may have come from an alien source. In my research, I stumbled across some classified documents that seem to indicate extraterrestrial influence, though I couldn't prove anything. You must try to destroy this weapon and rebuild the world as a better place, where the need for such technology no longer exists. And if anyone meets a thirteen-year-old girl named Sara Gunderson, please tell her I love her and I'm sorry."*

The woman sniffled, sounding like she struggled to keep from crying. She cleared her throat and added, *"This message will repeat."*

Shane lowered the handset and stood, his knees trembling and his legs threatening to collapse under him. Looking from Steve to Tracy, he was frozen in silent shock for what seemed an eternity.

"How freaking stupid," Shane whispered.

"No dumber than a nuke," Steve replied, reaching down and clicking the radio off. "Something like this was bound to happen eventually. Did you hear what she said? Do you think the government has really been in contact with aliens?"

"Why not? I'd believe anything at this point. What do you think the chances are that someone else heard this and is trying to shut the weapon down?" Shane asked, doing his best to stay calm and rational, though freaking out seemed completely appropriate considering the circumstances.

"Who knows?" Steve replied, shrugging his shoulders. "Someone would have had to take the time to scour the radio frequencies with a military radio like I've done. Seems very unlikely." He acted calmer than Shane or Tracy, his big shoulders slumped forward in defeat, appearing ready to throw in the towel and just quit trying to survive.

"I think we have to assume we are the only ones who heard this," Tracy said, her brow crinkled with frustration. "We have to get down there and shut that stupid thing off."

"Yeah, and soon," Shane added, glad she was thinking the same thing. "It sounds like the animals could go after us any minute. What did she say? They would attack younger and younger people every twenty-four to forty-eight hours?"

Shane glanced at the buses where Kelly slept. She was a year older than he was—the animals would go after her first. He'd taken care of her this far—he wasn't going to lose her now.

"Wake Aaron," Shane said, the purpose pushing him forward from the time she had walked down her driveway calling for his help made him square up and get motivated once again. "We leave immediately."

CHAPTER
TWENTY-THREE

"The buses are useless," Tracy announced, her fists on her hips.

Her stoic manner and tone took over, and though her brow still showed frustration and anger, the post-apocalyptic-super-survivor version of Tracy Shane was introduced to yesterday returned.

The dawn's light waxed, revealing the damage caused by the storm. Thick, glowing, lime-green clouds hung low overhead, the wind kicking up again. The three school buses suffered a lot of damage. They had flat tires, busted windows, and one had a steel beam sticking out of its front grill, a testament to the power of the tornado.

"I don't think walking is such a good idea either," Shane replied, scanning the base for another means of transportation. "Why don't you take Aaron and scout the area? Maybe y'all can find a couple of military trucks that are still in one piece."

"Yeah, a Humvee would be a hell of a lot cooler than a school bus," Aaron said. He'd crawled out from under the

Freightliners and was relieving himself nearby. "Where we going?"

"Yuck," Tracy growled. "There's got to be a better place to do that!"

"You're just jealous you can't whip it out and whiz wherever you please," Aaron countered, spinning around and zipping his pants with his hips thrust forward.

"Come on, guys," Shane scolded. "Can it, and find us some rides. Tracy will relay what we heard on the radio while you search."

"Yes sir," Aaron replied, giving a mock salute. As fresh as it was to see him acting in good spirits, his joking around didn't fool Shane. His eyes spoke of the pain they all felt, the loss of their parents still too recent an insult.

Aaron scooped his bow and quiver of arrows. Tracy and he set across the tarmac, dodging twisted remains of buildings and cars crumpled like stepped-on soda cans and dropped by the twister. The sounds of gunshots and mortar explosions carrying across the base yesterday were gone. All the soldiers must have killed each other, the animals wiping out the few who survived the battle.

Looking at the devastation, Shane was once again amazed they managed to survive. He took it as a sign. If they persisted, they might make it through this nightmare and stop the weapon before it killed them all.

Kids woke up and crawled out one by one from under the wet refuge. The curious little ones began poking around in the trash deposited by the tornado, and some of the older kids passed out the snacks and sodas that survived the night in the supply bus.

"Shane," Kelly called from under the bus with a distressed voice. "I think you'd better come here."

He dropped to his knees and reluctantly crawled into the wet shelter where he'd spent the night. Kelly crouched near the rear axle, leaning over Matt. Shane made his way back to her, careful not to bang his head on the driveshaft.

"What's up?"

"I don't think he's breathing," Kelly whispered. A tear dripped off her cheek and onto Matt's pale face.

Shane put his fingers on Matt's neck and didn't find a pulse. He knew as soon as he touched Matt's cold skin he was dead. Pulling the blanket back, a subtle odor of decaying flesh met Shane's nose. Nauseous, he laid his head on Matt's chest, listening for a heartbeat. He couldn't hear anything. Under Matt's half open eyelids, Shane could see the whites of his eyes looked dry and sticky.

He leaned back and pulled the blanket over Matt's head. Then Shane looked at Kelly, whose chin crinkled against a deluge of tears. Shane shook his head to let her know Matt had passed. She grabbed him and buried her face in his shirt, muffling her weeping.

Shane cradled her head with his hand, each of her sobs hot bullets searing through his otherwise-numb heart.

"It's better this way," Shane whispered. "He's not in pain anymore."

It sounded awkward and stupid, and he knew it would be better to be alive and in pain than dead, but Shane had to say something. The worst part was he didn't want to cry. And he and Matt were best friends when they were little. Shane couldn't feel anything except for a desire to save Kelly and to see her smile like she used to every day at school or at church. It was the only thing still anchoring his soul in his body. If he lost that thread of motivation, he may as well be dead himself.

"Come on," he said, wanting to get her away from Matt's corpse. "Let's get out of here."

"But," Kelly pulled away, wiping her eyes with the backs of her hands. "What do we do with him?"

"I think we should leave him here for now," Shane replied, hoping not to sound insensitive. "I don't want to upset the little kids."

Kelly nodded. They crawled out together. Natalie came over after they stood. She wore a blanket draped around her shoulders, the soggy and dirty bottom dragging the ground.

"I want to go home now," she said, peering up at Shane as if he was the reason she couldn't.

Shane glanced at Kelly, at a loss for words.

"Uh," Kelly stammered, "we can't just yet." Her voice sounded weak and unconvincing.

"Yeah," Shane added, trying to rescue Kelly. "The adventure isn't over."

"But this isn't any fun at all," Nat said, her green eyes big and wet and her chin crinkling.

"Come on," Kelly said, putting her hands on the little girl's shoulders and steering her away. "Let's get you some breakfast."

After watching Kelly and Nat, Shane took a deep

shaky breath and gazed across the tarmac. Matt's death hadn't affected him as he would expect, but the sad expression on that six-year-old girl's face caused him unbearable heartache. He couldn't imagine what would happen if the little ones didn't have the older kids to take care of them. They had to shut the weapon down and get the world back to normal, and they had to hurry.

A flock of crows flew overhead, screeching angrily at each other. Shane eyed them, worried. Any moment, the weapon could cause them to attack Kelly, and then shortly thereafter, Shane, Tracy, Steve, and Aaron would be targeted. If they didn't shut the weapon down before that happened, he doubted there'd be a kid left old enough to do it.

CHAPTER
TWENTY-FOUR

Shane put the kids to the task of gathering salvageable materials and supplies scattered by the storm and had Laura and Kelly listen to the scientist's radio broadcast. A grumbling sound carried across the tarmac, catching Shane's attention. A green army vehicle with a raised, boat-bow front end rolled toward him. It had eight wheels on four axles, a machine gun on top, and slits for windows.

He started to order the kids to crawl under the buses for cover, but a hatch on top of the angular vehicle flipped open and Aaron popped up and waved at him.

Looking like it could climb straight up a tree, the vehicle pulled in front of Shane and stopped. A hydraulic pump whined, and the rear gate on the machine lowered down to make a ramp. Tracy and Aaron climbed out.

"This should do the trick." Tracy almost beamed, though her tone was dispirited.

"What the heck is it?" Shane asked, studying the fierce vehicle.

"It's a Stryker armored personnel carrier," Tracy

announced. "That's a 12.7 mm machine gun on top, and those little tubes are grenade launchers. This baby should get us downtown—no problem."

"Check this out," Aaron said, waving Shane to the back of the Stryker.

Shane followed him up the ramp and into the belly of the machine.

"We found a bunch of guns and ammo." Aaron showed him weapons stacked on the bench seats on either side of the Stryker.

"What's that?" Shane pointed at blood spattering the walls.

"A couple of soldiers killed each other in here," Tracy said curtly, seeming annoyed Shane would complain. "We cleaned up the mess the best we could."

"It's a reminder we might do the same if we don't hurry," Shane whispered. He surveyed the rest of the interior and added, "This thing doesn't look like it'll carry too many people. What about all those kids we're responsible for?"

"We can't take them with us," Tracy answered, like it should have been apparent. "They'll slow us down anyway."

"What are we supposed to do?" He struggled to keep his anger in check. Tracy didn't act like she had a heart half the time. She seemed to be looking for a way to ditch the kids. "We've brought them this far—we can't just abandon them."

"They'll be safer here," Aaron said from behind Shane. "Once we get down to Atlanta, we're bound to find some trouble. Even if the buses would run, they won't protect those kids."

Did it make sense to leave the kids here on the base? It seemed somewhat safe and isolated. If all went as planned, they'd be back by nightfall. But the thought of abandoning them still made Shane uneasy.

"Do you know how to use these?" Shane asked, picking up a rifle.

"That's an M-16," Tracy replied. "And yes, I know how to use it. My dad got my JROTC unit access to the base's shooting range a few times." Tracy's stoic face twitched, pain in her eyes.

It was the first time she mentioned her dad since they left the high school, heading to this base to find him. He had to be dead, just like all of the other adults. Shane again felt the urge to say something to comfort Tracy, but she seemed so tough that he feared anything he'd come up with would sound too awkward and would probably tick her off, so he kept quiet.

"Take a few of these guns and show some of the older kids who won't be coming with us how to shoot them," Shane ordered, putting the M-16 in her hands. "And leave them plenty of ammo. They'll need it for protection while we're gone."

Tracy took the gun and nodded. Steve grabbed three more, carrying them to the kids who Kelly and Laura organized into two work groups. Shane had seen many types of guns growing up, most of them designed for hunting. But these, with their plastic stalks and black barrels, were made for one thing—killing people. In fact, he thought, glancing at a splatter of dried blood on the Stryker, these weapons had just killed people.

He jogged over and tried to find distraction in helping Kelly move sheet metal, the remains of the hanger, together to create lean-to shelters. Tracy took eight of the older girls behind the buses to give them a crash course on how to use the M-16s. Their eyes were wide with trepidation and missing any spark. He knew, especially after what they'd been through, they'd be able to defend themselves with the guns if they had to. Shane, Tracy, Steve, Kelly, and Aaron had already killed. He'd never get the images of those dying boys out of his head.

Once the shelters were finished, he helped Steve and Aaron gather supplies and stock the Stryker for the trip downtown. Shane called a meeting of the other four who had fought in the gym and Laura.

"We've all listened to the radio message," Shane said, looking at each of his friends and hoping to channel Coach Rice once again. "We know we have to get downtown and shut the weapon off."

Shane didn't really have a plan. He hoped someone else would jump in, and their silence said they expected him to have the answers. He'd always dreamed of being a quarterback, but not when the life or death of the rest of the people on the planet was at stake.

"Tracy and Aaron found us this armored truck, which should keep us safe if we run into trouble," Shane continued, patting the front of the Stryker. "Does anyone know how to get to the capitol building from here?"

"The Stryker is loaded with electronic maps, and it has GPS," Tracy said. "We won't have a problem finding our way."

"What about all those kids?" Kelly asked, glancing over her shoulder at the groups huddled thirty feet behind her.

Shane expected the question. He looked at Tracy and then Aaron, hoping one of them would give Kelly the news. Of course, they didn't answer.

"We're going to have to leave them here," Shane said, hoping he hadn't just started a fight.

"What?" Laura asked, sounding flabbergasted and glaring at him.

"We can't do that," Kelly retorted. "Most of them are too young—they won't be safe."

"Tracy taught some of the older girls to use the guns." Shane hated how the two girls had him backed in a corner. It wasn't like this was all his doing. "You guys are free to stay here too, but we need all the help we can get."

"Whose we?" Laura asked, glaring at each of them as if they'd been conspiring.

"I'm going," Tracy said, the usual coolness in her voice. She didn't break her gaze from Shane, barely acknowledging Laura's complaint. "I'm driving the Stryker."

"Me too," Steve chimed in, leaning back as if he were trying to hide behind Tracy.

"I'm the best shot here," Aaron said, obviousness in his tone, "so I have to go."

Shane figured it was pretty apparent he had to join the mission because no one else seemed to want to lead it.

"We need you two as well," Tracy said. She was the only one who didn't seem intimidated by the angry girls. "It might get ugly down there, and the more people we have, the better our chances."

"And in a few hours, the animals might be attacking us anyway," Steve said, poking his head out from behind Tracy. "We won't be much help to these kids if we stick around."

"I understand if you can't come along, Kelly," Shane said, "being that your little sister is here."

Kelly looked over her shoulder at the group of kids huddled near a small fire built in front of the lean-to shelters. After a moment, she returned her focus to Shane. Her blue eyes had always seemed to glow, emitting a constant flow of joy that made him blush when she looked at him. His chest ached to see so much sadness and pain in her gaze now. With her staring at him, deciding if she should leave her little sister behind, Shane made a silent vow that after all this was over, and the weapon had been shut down, he'd find a way to make Kelly happy once again—he'd find a way to make her smile.

"I have to go," she whispered. "I'm the oldest, so the animals will come after me first. It's better if I say goodbye to her now than have her see me ripped apart like… like…" She looked at the ground.

"Okay," Shane said, rescuing her before she could say, *like her parents*. He cleared his throat and clapped his hands together. "Let's say our goodbyes and get going. The sooner we shut that weapon down, the sooner we can get back here and make sure these kids stay safe."

CHAPTER
TWENTY-FIVE

Shane watched Kelly slowly walk over to the group of kids and sit down beside her little sister. He couldn't imagine how hard the conversation she was about to have must be. There was little he could do to help her. He joined Aaron in scrubbing the rest of the blood off the Stryker, wondering how long until he and his friends started killing each other like these soldiers had done. The M-16 on the seat in front of him would make the end come fast, not that it was much conciliation, but he preferred going by bullet instead of arrow or the blade of a knife. Kelly stepped into view at the rear hatch of the vehicle, her eyes moist with tears.

"How'd it go?" Shane asked.

"I told her I had work, that I'd just be gone for the day," Kelly replied, sniffling. "She didn't seem to care." She let out a pained chuckle. "As usual, she's dealing with all this better than I am."

"She'll be fine here," Shane said, putting his arms around Kelly and giving her a quick hug. "And, if all goes as planned, we'll be back by tonight, like you said."

"I sure hope so," Kelly replied. "I hope you don't mind, but I convinced Laura to stay here. The other kids need someone older to watch out for them, and she's younger than me so the weapon won't get to her right away."

"Sounds like a good idea," Shane agreed. Tracy and Laura were always at each other's throats anyway, and the trip would be easier if he didn't have to play referee between them.

The Stryker's engine grumbled to life, and Kelly and Shane climbed in the back with Aaron and Steve. Tracy was up front in the driver's seat. Steve closed the rear hatch, and the Stryker lurched forward, almost throwing Shane off his bench.

"Sorry," Tracy yelled over the noisy diesel. "She's a bit touchy."

It took Tracy several miles to master operating the heavy vehicle. While they bounced along, Aaron showed everyone how to use the M-16s, and then they changed into fresh clothing. Kelly faced forward and the boys faced the rear to give her some privacy. Putting on the bulletproof vest and helmet Tracy and Aaron retrieved from the dead soldiers, Shane was careful not to study the camouflaged material too closely, fearing some of the splotches of dark belonged to the prior owner. He stood on the bench, sticking his head and shoulders up out of the Stryker's rear hatch. Wearing the same protective gear, Kelly rose up through the hatch next to him, and Steve stood through the gunner's hatch in the middle of the armored vehicle, manning the machine gun mounted on the roof.

They rolled through an upper middle-class

neighborhood with large homes on either side of the street. The yards were well kept, covered in lush, green grass, and the houses had flower gardens in full bloom, some with the stars and stripes and the Georgia state flag hanging from their porches.

Everything looked peaceful, tidy, and normal—except for the dead bodies.

A two-story red brick house with white pillars supporting the roof over the front porch had a middle-aged woman and an older woman laying near the flowerbeds, presumably a mother and her daughter. Their large, matching straw sunhats lay next to them, and a plastic tray of flowers sat in the grass nearby, ready to plant. The older woman had a gardening spade sticking out of her chest, and her daughter had the spike of a sprinkler head protruding from her eye.

Shane glanced at Kelly, knowing he'd never get the horrible image out of his brain. Had these poor people been driven insane when they attacked each other, oblivious? Or worse, were they conscious of what they were doing, yet unable to stop themselves? She put a hand on his forearm and squeezed, then returned her somber gaze to the passing houses.

He worried some of these houses might harbor children who were too young to get out or take care of themselves. The Stryker's engine was loud enough to drown out any other noise, but he wondered if the screams of starving babies would fill the air in the absence of the deafening diesel. He felt guilty for not stopping to investigate, but at this moment, they had to keep going. The children would certainly die if they didn't shut down the weapon. They could come back and investigate afterwards, though he knew he and his friends didn't have the resources to care for any more kids than they were already responsible for. He could only hope other teenagers were taking responsibility for the youngsters who had lost their parents. Right now, he had to stay focused, or everyone was doomed.

Two blocks away, a man in a business suit lay facedown in his driveway, a pistol on the bloody ground next to him. The next house had a woman in the yard, a shotgun next to her and a dark red spot covering her chest. Shane tried not to look at any more of the bodies, focusing his attention on the road ahead. It didn't help much, because there were dead adults littering the streets as well. Some of them looked mangled, their bodies bent in unnatural ways, run over by psychos who mowed people down with their cars. Others were shot, and more bludgeoned with gardening tools and household items like the mother and daughter Shane saw at the other end of the street. And there were mutilated bodies, most likely torn apart by crazed neighborhood dogs or wild animals.

The Stryker rolled out of the neighborhood and onto a main road lined with businesses. The buildings grew taller with each passing block, and the number of the dead on the streets increased. Shane knew they must be getting closer to the capitol building, praying it would stay this quiet all the way there.

A movement to the left caught Shane's attention. He looked down the side street and saw a motorcycle zip through the intersection. Its rider's helmetless head turned, looking at Shane just before the bike disappeared between buildings.

"Someone's following us," Shane yelled to Kelly and then leaned forward and told Steve, pointing down the street at the next light.

Steve nodded, and climbed down into the Stryker. He popped up with two M-16s, handing one to Shane and one to Kelly. She took the weapon and looked at Shane with concern.

"Don't worry," Shane yelled confidently in her ear. "They won't dare mess with us while we're in this beast." He patted the armored, green roof of their rolling fortress.

Each intersection they passed, Shane glanced down the side streets and saw more motorcycles shadowing them. And then Tracy slowed the Stryker. A blockade of cars with a bunch of teenagers standing in front of it obstructed the road ahead. Shane tried to count them, guessing there were over a hundred. They all held guns, but at least they weren't pointing them at the approaching Stryker. He felt a surge of hope. If they could get this army of kids on their side, then disabling the Limbic Manipulator Weapon might be an easy task.

Tracy brought the Stryker to a halt fifty feet from the blockade. Steve manned the machine gun mounted on the roof, and Kelly held her M-16 ready. Shane remembered how he used to think she was so feminine and sweet. Now he saw her differently. After all, she killed some of the escaped inmates who attacked the girls in the gym. And now, her gentle and caring expression was replaced by the steely look of a soldier, ready and willing to fight. The gun in her hands and her helmet and body armor made her look even tougher.

Shane left his M-16 laying on the roof of the Stryker, crawled up out of his hatch, and sat down next to Steve's machine gun, attempting to make it clear he wanted to talk and did not plan to immediately attack.

The teens pushed closer together, and he worried one of them might get too excited and start shooting. In the front of the pack, a thick kid with a slight grin and malice in his eyes started to raise the shotgun in his hands but a taller boy, Shane guessed to be about seventeen years old, put his hand on the barrel and pushed it down. The tall boy's eyes never left Shane, and with the way the thick kid obeyed, it was clear who the leader was.

Once Tracy killed the Stryker's diesel engine, tense quiet fell over the street. Shane had been to downtown Atlanta a few times, and he was certain it was never so quiet. The hot breeze whispered between the sharp corners and flat faces of the towering buildings, warning of the fragility of the momentary peace.

"Nice toy you got there," the tall guy in the middle of the group shouted. "Where y'all headed in such a hurry?" Shane noted he had a black police utility belt around his waist with a gun holstered on it.

"Downtown," Shane replied firmly, while also trying to keep threat out of his voice. "Would you please be so kind as to step aside and let us pass?"

The guy smiled, revealing a gold grill over his upper teeth. He rested his arm on the smaller kid next to him, who held the shotgun.

"Name's Shamus," the tall guy said. "Downtown is my

jurisdiction. Nobody passes without my permission."

"Great," Shane replied, still hopeful this could work out. "Maybe you can help us."

"Oh, we'd be glad to help you," Shamus mocked. A chuckle passed through his large and intimidating gang. "Just exactly what would we be helping you with?"

Shane glanced at Steve, who had the Stryker's machine gun trained on Shamus. Steve shrugged as if to say, *Tell them everything—maybe they will help us.* Shane decided they had nothing to lose, and he sure as heck didn't want to have a shootout with these kids, even if the armored vehicle put the odds in his favor.

"We know why the animals killed the adults and why the adults attacked each other," Shane began. "There's a top secret weapon downtown causing all this to happen." Shane paused and tried to read Shamus, whose golden smile reflected the dim sunlight passing through the thick, green clouds overhead. The city was eerily silent as they stared at each other, and yet the tension made the quiet seem to roar.

"Go on," Shamus said.

"Well," Shane continued, "we're gonna shut it down."

Shamus' eyes narrowed. He pulled at the scruffy, dark goatee growing on his chin. After a moment, he said, "No."

"Uh… what do you mean, *no?*" Shane asked, resisting the urge to reach back and grab his rifle.

"I mean, no, you ain't going downtown to shut the weapon off," Shamus replied, his tone ominous and threatening, though the malicious grin never left his face. He stood straighter and put his hand on the pistol strapped to his waist. "You see, ever since the animals and the adults went crazy, we've been living like kings. We own this city now, and we ain't planning on stepping down from our throne any time soon."

"But you don't understand," Shane said, trying to salvage the negotiation. "The weapon is going to cause the animals to go after younger and younger people soon. Any moment now, you could be attacked, or you guys will turn on each other like the adults did."

"Yeah? I ain't buying it," Shamus said casually, slipping his pistol out of its holster. He crossed his arms over his chest, the barrel of his gun resting over his elbow. "Now turn this thing around and get out of my city. Get on back to your fantasyland, talk'n secret weapons and such. What's next, we're gonna be jumped by a bunch of unicorns?"

The gang laughed at their leader's joke. Shane heard a nervous undertone in their chuckles, and several of them glanced at their weapons, perhaps shifting the safeties off. Not wanting to appear intimidated, he stared at the tall and skinny kid for a long moment, deciding what to do next. Steve could probably mow most of them down with the machine gun in a matter of seconds, but Shane didn't have the stomach to order their execution.

"Alright," Shane said, holding his hands up in defeat. "Suit yourselves. We'll leave."

CHAPTER
TWENTY-SIX

Steve gave Shane a, *What the heck* look. Shane put a hand on his shoulder and shook his head. Then he dropped through the hatch into the Stryker and crawled forward to where Tracy sat, in the driver's seat.

"Turn it around," Shane ordered, hoping he was doing the right thing.

"We can't let these punks stop us," Tracy snapped. "We got them out gunned, and their bullets can't even penetrate our armor."

"Yeah, but I'm not ready to slaughter them," Shane countered. "Are you?"

"Well no—of course not," Tracy replied. It seemed she hadn't thought about the fact that they might have to kill a bunch of kids. Her brow furrowed and she blinked her eyes, refocusing on Shane. "But we have to get down there and shut the weapon off."

"And we will," Shane replied. "Just turn around, and we'll drive a few blocks away, then take a different route."

"Okay," Tracy said, reluctance clear in her voice. "But

you know they're gonna come after us when we turn back."

"Not if we can steer far enough around them." Shane feared she was right, but they couldn't just start shooting—they had to at least try to avoid a fight.

Tracy started the diesel and backed up a block. When she was well clear of the thugs, she caused the tires to rotate in different directions, pivoting the machine one hundred and eighty degrees so fast it made him dizzy. The Stryker lurched north. Shane grabbed his M-16 and stood through the hatch, worried the gang would attack the rear of the vehicle as they drove away. Still holding his gun in one hand, Shamus waved at him, smiling broadly with his gold teeth.

They drove over a hill and out of sight. Then Shane dropped inside and told Tracy to turn left and go ten blocks before heading downtown.

"You know they'll still catch up with us," Aaron yelled, reiterating Tracy's warning when Shane sat down on the Stryker's bench seating across from him.

"I think we'll have a better chance of busting through them. They won't have time to set up a barricade," Shane replied, agitated by how both Tracy and Aaron naysaid his ideas but didn't offer any other options.

What they would do once they made it past the thugs, Shane hadn't figured out yet. It was going to be hard to get out of the Stryker at the capitol building if an angry mob surrounded them.

He crawled forward and looked at the GPS—four miles to the capitol building. Not very far, but Shane expected it would be the roughest drive he'd ever take in his life.

"Better go topside," Tracy said. "Just saw a motorcycle cross the intersection up ahead."

"If we run into any trouble, just keep driving," Shane ordered. "Don't stop until we make it to the capitol."

"Got it," Tracy replied.

Shane took a deep breath and crawled to the rear of the Stryker. He tapped Aaron on the shoulder and pointed at Kelly. "Take her place."

Aaron nodded. Shane climbed on the bench and stood up through the hatch next to Kelly.

"I need you to go below," he yelled.

"Why?" Kelly asked, her forehead crinkling in confusion. "I'm fine here."

"Please."

"What, you don't think I can fight?"

"It's not that," Shane stammered. He'd insulted her, not his intention. "It's just that…" Shane couldn't find the words.

"Fine," she shouted louder than necessary to be heard over the roar of the Stryker's diesel engine. She glared at him and dropped below.

Aaron popped up a moment later, giving Shane a, *What did you say to her* look. Shane shook his head and picked up his M-16. Kelly proved herself in action; she could hold her own. His behavior was as much of a surprise to him as he supposed it was to her. It was an instinctive action to send her below, done without premeditation. He didn't care if he got killed, but he couldn't stand the idea of her getting hurt. Whether she hated him for it or not, that couldn't happen while he was alive.

"Heads up!" Steve yelled, pointing in the direction they headed. He hadn't moved from his position on the Stryker's machine gun since they entered the city.

Shane leaned forward and saw a group of motorcycles cross an intersection two blocks down. He glanced at Aaron, clicked the safety off on his gun, and saw him do the same. They went three more blocks, Tracy swerving around deserted cars so fast that Shane got slammed against the edges of the hatch, adrenaline masking the pain of the bruises he sustained to his ribs through his bulletproof vest.

They swerved through another intersection. Shane glanced left in time to see the word MACK on the chrome grill of a dump truck, the shiny, little bulldog hood ornament glaring down at him. It slammed into the side of the Stryker, knocking Shane off the bench, making him fall down the hatch and into the armored vehicle. He blinked in the dim interior, stunned. Kelly lay crumpled on the floor in front of him. The dump truck hit them so hard that it caused the Stryker's engine to stall.

"You okay?" she groaned. A red stream flowed away from her split open lip.

"I'm fine—what about you?" Shane wiped blood off her chin with his thumb.

A deafening explosion went off before she had a chance to answer. It sounded like it came from beneath them and felt like the Stryker jumped into the air and slammed back down onto the asphalt. When the armored vehicle came to a rest, Shane scrambled to his feet and rose up out of the hatch, his M-16 ready. Aaron and Steve dumped rounds into the street behind the dump truck, and Shane heard pings and saw flashes as kids hiding behind cars returned fire. The Mack truck idled sickly just behind the Stryker, its front end smashed and its driver leaning forward with blood running down his face from a hole in his temple, a precision kill no doubt delivered by Aaron.

Steve pumped rounds out of his machine gun, yelling the entire time. Aaron had an eerily calm look on his face, like he was in the woods hunting deer. He lined up his sights on a target, smoothly pulled the trigger, and then shifted his gun to the next target, not waiting to see if the bullet hit its mark. A boy fifty yards out dropped.

Before Shane could level his weapon, the armored vehicle's diesel engine grumbled to life. Tracy pulled the Stryker forward through the intersection. Shane couldn't see the damage the dump truck caused, but the Stryker still seemed to be working fine at the moment. There was a large hole in the road and charred marks where the explosion occurred, and Shane realized the thugs must've set off some kind of bomb under the Stryker after they'd hit it with the Mack truck. Sparks erupted where a bullet ricocheted off the metal hatch next to him. Without really aiming, Shane returned fire at the cars where he saw puffs of smoke from the gangsters' guns.

"Use short bursts," Aaron shouted, slamming a new clip into his M-16. "We have to save our ammo."

Steve clearly didn't hear Aaron's advice, still yelling and spraying bullets. Tracy got them across the intersection and onto the next block. The Stryker's engine roared, and she drove it up onto the sidewalk to get around the cars blocking the road.

A flash came from inside the darkness of a second floor window of a building they passed, and Shane felt a sharp burn across the side of his neck. He put his hand up to the spot and felt something wet.

"You've been hit!" Aaron yelled.

"Hit?" It took a second for it to register—he had been shot.

"Go below," Aaron said, his expression full of concern.

The Stryker pulled through the next intersection, and a barrage of gunfire made Shane duck inside before he could respond. Aaron and Steve dropped inside to take cover as well.

"Close the hatches," Kelly yelled over the pinging of bullets hitting the vehicle's armor. "Stay inside. We can shoot out of these little holes."

Shane reached up and pulled his hatch closed, as did Aaron and Steve, muffling the sound of the guns outside. But when the bullets hit the Stryker, it sounded like they were inside a drum. Kelly shoved the barrel of her M-16 out of a gun port, and fired. His ears felt like someone set firecrackers off in them. Shane slid a narrow port open next to Kelly and put his gun through it. When he pulled the trigger, the gun's report didn't seem as loud, he assumed because he was going deaf.

Taking aim at a boy who held a shotgun on his waist about fifty feet from the Stryker, Shane pulled the trigger. He could see the boy's eyes go wide, the fierce look on his face replaced by a limp expression of shock. Dropping the shotgun, the boy stood for a moment, an eternity for Shane. He seemed to stare into Shane's eyes, suddenly appearing young and innocent. Then the boy dropped dead to the asphalt.

The boy's slack expression seared itself onto the inside of Shane's eyelids. Every time he blinked, the dying, young face was there, staring blankly at him. Shane's rifle clicked— its clip empty. Unable to focus on another target, he pulled the barrel out of the gun port and slid the narrow door closed.

Sitting back on the bench on the opposite side of the Stryker, he gritted his teeth to hold back a surge of vomit. When he'd shot the juvenile delinquent in the gym with his crossbow, he hadn't seen his face like that of the boy he'd just killed. And this kid looked so innocent just before he died; maybe he'd never really done anything wrong to deserve getting shot. How many good kids had been recruited by Shamus, kids who had the same reservations about killing that Shane did? Maybe they had nowhere else to turn, or the gangster didn't give them an option.

Knowing he had to keep fighting, Shane crawled forward toward the green, canvas bag filled with M-16 clips sitting just behind Tracy. His ears ringing, he couldn't hear very well, but he felt a disturbing change in the vibration coming from the diesel and knew something was off. He leaned over Tracy's shoulder and saw the oil pressure dropping to almost nothing and the engine temperature climbing into the red.

"The engine must've taken a hit," Shane yelled into her ear. "It won't make it much longer."

"What do you want me to do?" Tracy asked. Her expression frantic, sweat drenched her face as she jerked the steering wheel back and forth to get around obstacles in the road.

Looking out the slit of bulletproof glass that comprised the windshield, Shane could see Shamus' gangsters running ahead of the Stryker, ducking into buildings and shooting at the armored vehicle. There had to be hundreds. If they broke down here, the gangsters would encircle them, wait until they used up all their ammo, and then crawl all over the Stryker until they found a way to break in.

"Get us out of here," he ordered.

"What?" Tracy glanced back. "Shouldn't we just plow through and try to make it to the capitol building?"

"We'll never make it," Shane replied, giving in to his instincts. "We have to lose these guys before our engine dies. Turn us around. Now!"

Tracy looked at him again, like she planned to object. But his expression must've convinced her, because at the next intersection, she spun the heavy vehicle around and gunned the engine. After heading a few blocks in the opposite direction, the pings of bullets hitting the armored hull diminished and then stopped altogether, the thugs seeming satisfied they had won the fight.

Kelly leaned back from her porthole with a confused expression on her face. She crawled over and shouted into Shane's ear. "What happened? Why did we turn back?"

As if to answer, a loud, banging noise came from the diesel and an acrid stench filled the cabin. Shane knew the smell all too well. It was the odor of metal grinding against metal. There was no oil left in the engine to lubricate or cool it. The smell meant the overheated engine was about to seize.

CHAPTER TWENTY-SEVEN

The armored vehicle limped along for a few more blocks before a loud thunk came from the engine compartment, followed by grinding. The Stryker jerked to a stop, and silence fell over the interior, seeming thick enough to drown them after all the noise of battle.

"Damn," Tracy hissed. The ignition system whined a couple of times. She tried to get the diesel restarted.

"It's seized," Shane told her. "The only way this beast is going anywhere is with a new engine."

"Why the hell did we turn around?" Steve asked, sounding frustrated.

"If we hadn't, we'd be stuck down there with all those thugs trying to peel this thing open and get at us," Aaron answered before Shane had a chance. "Or worse, they might have lit the Stryker on fire and cooked us in it if we refused to come out."

"Too bad," Kelly said, leaning her head back and looking at the ceiling. "We had to be so close."

"Yeah," Tracy agreed, climbing out of the driver's seat

and back into the passenger compartment. "We only had about two miles to go."

"What now?" Aaron asked, looking at Shane.

"Now we get the heck out of this coffin before they come to see if we left town," Shane said, trying to sound like he had a plan.

The truth was, he didn't have a clue what to do next. But his four friends looked at him like they'd fall apart if he didn't have the answers. As soon as he gave an order, a subtle look of relief came over their faces, and they grabbed their weapons and gear, climbing toward the rear hatch of the Stryker. His football coach told him once that he had the makings of a great leader, that he just needed the right circumstances to bring it out.

Too bad this hell was what it took.

The last one out of the Stryker, Shane raised his M-16 to his shoulder and took up position on the left side of the smoking vehicle, pointing down the street from which they'd just come. The others had done the same, all acting like he guessed seasoned soldiers would in the same situation. Again, he sensed they awaited his orders.

He glanced around, trying to think of the best move. The sound of motorcycles approaching from the south jolted him into action.

"Let's take cover in there," he waved his gun barrel at a ten-story building with a granite façade. "Quickly."

Shane jogged behind the others, keeping his gun trained down the street. They made it into the building before he saw the motorcycles. He led the way up to the third floor, and they positioned themselves by the windows, aiming their guns down into the street.

"Stay in the shadows," Tracy whispered, "so they won't see us if they look up."

The motorcycles' drone grew louder, and then they appeared on the street below. Shane counted fifteen, but more could have been close to the building or down the block. They came to a stop around the Stryker and killed their engines. With guns aiming at the armored vehicle, they surrounded it and peered in the back door.

"It's empty," a boy shouted.

"They must've taken off on foot," another said.

"Should we go after them?"

"Naw—this is Maurice's territory. He'll deal with them."

"Yeah. Let's get out of here before Maurice's lackeys try to deal with us."

"I ain't scared. You scared?"

"Shut up, numb nuts, or I'll show you scared."

"Both of y'all shut up before I bust a cap in ya," a deeper voice said. "Get on your bikes and ride."

"I know you didn't just say *bust a cap*," a boy spouted, the others cackling with him.

A few seconds later, the motorcycles roared to life, and the thugs headed back the way they'd come.

Exhaling slowly, Shane realized he'd been holding his breath the whole time the gangsters were on the street below.

"That was a bit too close," Kelly whispered.

Shane stepped nearer to the window and peered out.

"Looks clear now."

"What happened to your neck?" Kelly asked, her voice filled with concern.

"I guess a bullet grazed me." He reached up and felt the sticky blood, his wound stinging now that she mentioned it.

"Let me clean it up," Kelly said, pulling a small first aid kit out of her pocket.

"How do we get to the capitol building now?" Steve asked, discouraged.

"We walk," Shane replied, cringing as Kelly wiped his wound with alcohol swabs. "If we can go from building to building and keep quiet, I bet we can get past Shamus' gang without them noticing." He wasn't convinced, but they didn't have a choice. To give up meant waiting for the animals to attack and kill them.

"It would be better if we can get down there undetected and don't have to fight them off while we're trying to focus on shutting down the weapon," Aaron said, optimistic in spite of how dire things had gotten.

"Then it's agreed," Tracy said. "Let's get moving before the weapon makes us turn on each other."

Shane eyed the M-16 in each of his friends' hands, realizing how quickly it all would end if the limbic manipulator scrambled their brains. Kelly finished cleaning his wound, putting some antibiotic ointment and bandages on it, and he flashed a smile at her to say thanks, remembering she was the oldest and the first person to be affected by the weapon if it did shift its settings.

"Tracy's right," he said, rising to his feet. "Let's move."

CHAPTER
TWENTY-EIGHT

They followed Shane down the steps through the building, and then slipped outside behind him. He was surprised at how comfortable he felt about marching into the street and becoming the target for hundreds of angry and heavily armed teenage gangsters. The numbness he'd experienced in varying degrees since his aunt died had something to do with his tranquil state. But he had also accepted that getting to the capitol building was their only chance to survive. The other two courses their destiny could take would be death by being shot by gangsters, or death from the limbic manipulator weapon. His entire focus was on their one chance to stay alive. Knowing what needed to be done—even if their odds of success were one in a million—had an oddly calming effect on Shane.

"Shouldn't we go down another street?" Aaron asked after they darted into the next building.

"No," Tracy replied, glancing at Shane as if to see if he agreed. "I think we're better off going back down this one. They won't expect us to be stupid enough to do that, and it's a straight route to the capitol. We might get lost if we try to change our course."

Tracy looked as calm as Shane felt. He wondered if this is how she was all the time, even before the world got turned upside down. They'd only had a couple of classes together, and when he'd seen her at school, she always wore the same expression of seriousness and focus she displayed now. What had happened to her to make her so numb and emotionless? Regardless, he felt lucky she was here—a member of his team in this life-or-death game in which they found themselves.

Shane's foot caught on a body, and he almost tripped and fell on his face. All the buildings and the streets had corpses scattered everywhere—yet he'd become so jaded from seeing the dead he hardly noticed anymore. The bodies had begun to swell, and flies buzzed around them. Decay was setting in, and soon they'd start stinking.

"She's right. Let's keep moving," Shane said, trying not to think of how horrible it would be to be surrounded by a million rotting corpses.

Back out in the dim daylight, his small team pointed their guns in every direction and ran down the sidewalk. In the middle of the pack, Shane covered the opposite side of the street with Kelly at his back. They entered the next building, a fancy shopping mall with handbag stores bearing French names Shane couldn't pronounce. It was the kind of place where he guessed his aunt would've gone shopping. The thought sent a bolt of pain through his chest.

Leading the way out a door at the other end of the

mall, Shane saw a pack of dogs trotting down the street. A large Rottweiler led at least thirty others of all breeds. Holding his hand up, he stopped Kelly just before she stepped out. A pit-bull with a thick chain adorning its neck veered from the pack and paused, studying Shane. Bloodstains on the white fur around the dog's thick jaws told the story of how its owners must've died. It raised its head, its ribs pumping in and out as it smelled him. Shifting its attention to the right, the dog's brownish-gold eyes locked onto Kelly. The pit-bull let out a deep, rumbling growl, lowering its head and baring its teeth.

"Back off, dog," Shane threatened, raising the barrel of his gun and lining the sights up with the animal's big skull.

The dog crept toward Kelly, the white hair from its neck to its tail rising up into a long mohawk. From the corner of his eye, Shane saw Kelly stepping back. The dog barked, startling Shane such that he pulled the trigger. The gun's report echoed between the buildings, the pit-bull dropping dead with a gaping hole in its forehead.

"The weapon must be starting to make them target younger people," Tracy said worriedly, stepping beside Shane with her gun aimed at the pack of dogs.

Most of them tucked their tails between their hind legs and ran down the street, afraid of the gun. But a few stopped and gave curious looks toward the mall. Shane held his breath, his weapon pointed at the dogs. Seeming uninterested, they turned and continued trotting down the street, their heads held high like they owned the world. And Shane knew they did. If they all attacked at once, he expected he and his four friends couldn't hold them off for very long.

"At least the rest of them didn't come after us," Steve said, eyeing the dogs. "Maybe that one was just mean."

"Yeah, maybe," Shane replied, doubtful.

Aaron stepped onto the sidewalk. "We'd better hurry just the same."

Glancing at Kelly, Shane saw her face had lost all of its color.

"Don't worry," he said, putting his hand on her shoulder. "I won't let them get to you."

She gave a weak smile, whispering, "Thanks."

He slid his hand down her arm and laced his fingers through hers. Instead of pulling away, Kelly squeezed like she trusted he could keep her safe. He had to. If he could keep her alive, he believed things would work out—life at least stood a slim chance of being good again. Jogging along behind Tracy, he remembered how hopeless his best efforts were when his aunt was attacked. It reminded him he could do little if the insects and animals came after Kelly, but he still resolved to die before he let them hurt her.

They ducked into the next store, a ransacked coffee shop. A patron lay on the floor with a portion of the long, metal needle of the thermometer used to check to see if the drinks were the right temperature sticking out of his eye, piercing deep into his brain.

"Looks like he bitched about his latte one too many times," Steve mumbled, stepping over the body and grabbing a brownie off the shelf below the register.

"You think that's bad," Aaron said, chuckling behind

the counter. "Looks like the barista got beaten to death with a coffee carafe." He picked up a dented, stainless-steel container and waved it like he was threatening Steve. "I said half soy, no whip!" he shouted with mock anger.

"Come on, guys," Shane said, feeling like a jerk because he'd almost started laughing. "Don't be so disrespectful."

"Hey, man," Steve replied guiltily. "Just trying not to lose it."

"Something moved in the building across the street," Tracy said over her shoulder. Shane rushed to the front door where she had taken up guard. "Fourth window to the left of the corner, up on the third floor. The one with the planter box hanging off it." Tracy pointed her gun at the high-rise apartment building.

Shane didn't see anything besides a curtain billowing out of an open window. Aaron stepped on Tracy's other side.

"Your mind might be playing tricks on you," Aaron said.

"I know what I saw," Tracy retorted.

The volatility amongst the exhausted members of Shane's little team seemed to be increasing. And he knew it would only get worse, because they weren't going to get quality rest anytime soon.

"We'll keep our eyes peeled," Shane said, clapping Tracy on the shoulder. "Let's move, people."

The next block had a large parking structure on it that didn't offer much of a place to hide. They trotted in the open, guns held ready, with Shane leading the way. Halfway down the block, they crossed the structure's wide driveway.

"Yo," a male voice yelled from inside the parking structure. "Where y'all going in such a hurry?"

Spinning toward the sound, Shane raised his gun to his shoulder, pointing it into the dark interior of the garage.

"Who's there?" Shane asked, trying to sound intimidating.

"Let's move toward cover," Tracy whispered.

Giving a slight nod, Shane sidestepped to the right, and the other four did the same, all with their guns trained on the parking structure.

"No use in trying to get away," the deep voice shouted. "We got a whole grip of guns pointed at you."

"Show yourself," Shane replied, continuing to move toward the concrete wall alongside the entrance to the parking structure. He didn't see anybody with guns pointing at him and his friends, so he suspected the deep voice's owner might be bluffing.

"Gladly," the voice said. "Lower the business ends of your boom-sticks first. We ain't interested in acquiring any lead poisoning on this beautiful summer's afternoon."

Shane shot a look at the heavy, green clouds hanging low overhead. Not exactly what he'd call a nice day. He decided it couldn't be Shamus' people in the garage, or they would've already attacked. Hoping maybe they'd gain the ally they needed to help them get downtown, he lowered the barrel of his gun and motioned for the others to do the same. Tracy pointed hers at the ground last, giving Shane a look that said she wasn't convinced it was the right thing to do. A loud whistle came from inside the parking structure, and then the unsmiling faces of at least fifty kids rose up along the concrete barrier wall of the second floor.

Glancing over his shoulder, Shane saw a similar number of teenagers slipping out from behind cars and out of the office buildings across the street. They held guns, baseball bats, and a few even had machetes. A cold sense of dread settled over him. The voice wasn't bluffing, Shane and his friends were surrounded, and this time without the Stryker for protection.

CHAPTER
TWENTY-NINE

"Maurice?" Shane asked the short and stocky bronze-skinned teenager who stepped out from behind the parking lot attendant's booth sitting in the middle of the entrance to the garage.

"That I am." Maurice smiled in a way that made him seem friendly and threatening at the same time. "Have we met before, or does my reputation precede me?" He narrowed his eyes, studying Shane.

"Reputation," Shane admitted, trying to give the impression he believed he could take on the army of teens surrounding him and win. "Ran into some friends of yours downtown."

"Yes, so I heard. Y'all did quite the number on those criminals—it's amazing that y'all are alive," Maurice answered. Smiling broadly, he laid the barrel of his shotgun over his shoulder and walked closer. "Any enemy of Shamus is a friend of mine."

Taking Maurice's outstretched hand and shaking it, Shane studied the gang leader's brown eyes, trying to decide if he could trust him.

"Why do you guys hate each other?" Shane asked. He knew if he could get Maurice's army on his side, they'd have a much better chance of getting to the capitol building and shutting down the weapon. But Maurice could be just as bent on keeping things the way they were as Shamus. Having learned from his previous mistake of telling Shamus everything up front, Shane didn't want to risk divulging his plan until he learned more.

"Shamus is a gangster," Maurice said, reaching into the cargo pocket of his pants and pulling out an apple. "When the adults and animals went wack, Shamus and his gang of drug-dealing thugs recruited the smaller gangs and anyone else bent on wreaking havoc and took control of the downtown area almost immediately. Y'all wouldn't have made it out if it weren't for your toys." Maurice nodded at the gun in Shane's hands.

"So what are you guys trying to do?" Shane asked, keeping his face stoic and his voice firm. He didn't want to show any sign of weakness, feeling like the entire city was a giant tank full of hungry sharks.

"We're just trying to survive," Maurice answered sincerely, taking a bite of the apple. "After the world went to crap and Shamus' gang attacked and killed a few of us, we figured out that we'd have to band together to defend ourselves. We staked out this area of town as our own, and Shamus' gang has let us be since we started fighting back. Now, what about you? Why are you so bent on heading downtown?"

Looking from Kelly to Tracy and then to Steve and

Aaron, Shane tried to decide if he should come out with the truth. Kelly shrugged as if to say, *What do we have to lose*, and Tracy gave a little nod. The guys were too busy scanning the crowd of armed teenagers surrounding them to notice.

"The adults and animals went berserk because of a top-secret military weapon," he said, turning his attention on Maurice.

Narrowing his brown eyes, Maurice said, "Go on."

"We are trying to shut it down." Shane didn't want to say too much at once, figuring he could change the story if he didn't like Maurice's reaction.

"That would've been nice a couple of days ago," Maurice replied. "But it seems like the damage has already been done. What is the point of shutting it down now?"

"Well, things are gonna get worse. A lot worse," Shane said sternly. "We tried to explain this to Shamus, but he either didn't believe us or didn't care."

"Probably both," Maurice said, glowering down the street toward Shamus' territory. He looked back at Shane. "How do you know all this?"

"We picked up a message on a military radio. It was recorded by a scientist who helped make the weapon," Shane replied. He wasn't convinced Maurice had good intentions, but he liked the short, stocky guy a heck of a lot better than Shamus already. "The message said where the weapon is and how to shut it down."

"And it's obviously downtown." Maurice tossed his apple core into the bushes, wiped his hand on his pant leg, and then shifted his shotgun over to his other shoulder.

"Yep, under the Georgia Dome," Shane replied, not taking his eyes off Maurice's for even a second. "And the access to the weapon is through a tunnel that's in the capitol building."

Maurice scratched the chub hanging beneath his chin with his thick fingers. The stocky leader of the army of teens encircling them reminded Shane of a shorter, darker version of Steve. He studied Shane and his friends for a long moment.

"I'm afraid to ask," he said. "But what's gonna happen if we don't shut this weapon down?"

Upon hearing Maurice use the word *we*, Shane wanted to jump up and down and hug the jovial-looking kid. Knowing even if they did decide to help, these guys could back out at any moment, he contained his excitement the best he could. "The weapon will cause the animals to turn on us and us to turn on each other like the adults did."

"Great," Maurice said, rubbing his free hand across the bushy growth of hair atop his head. "And when is this going to happen?"

"Any moment. It might've already started." Shane glanced at Kelly, remembering how the dog tried to attack her. "So will you help us? We'd have a much better chance of getting downtown with you people on our side."

"Yeah, I'll help you," Maurice replied without hesitation. He looked around at the gun-toting kids comprising his gang. "But I'm not really the big boss here. We're just sticking together for protection. I'll try to get as many of these folks to help us as possible, but I can't make any promises."

"Thanks," Shane said, smiling gratefully.

Maurice nodded. He stepped a few feet away from Shane and his group, putting his hands up around his mouth to amplify his voice.

"Gather around people," he yelled, his booming voice so loud it sounded like he was speaking through a megaphone. "I got some important news to share with y'all."

The teenagers came down out of the parking garage, and even more exited from the buildings across the street, closing in around Maurice. They wore the expression of shellshock that Shane had seen on most kids' faces, like they'd all watched their parents die. Thinking back, he didn't recall seeing the sad expressions on the faces of many of the kids in Shamus' gang. They must've all come from families even more messed up than his own. The thought made him feel sorry for them and miss his dad at the same time.

Maurice spoke with an assertive tone, relaying all that Shane had told him. An impressive orator, Shane wondered if he might've become a politician or a preacher if the world Shane, and he reckoned everyone else, had taken for granted hadn't come to a swift and violent end.

Once Maurice told the kids about the secret weapon and explained that they'd have to fight their way through Shamus' gang to get downtown where they could shut it down, he paused for a long moment and pivoted around, seeming to look into the eyes of everyone there. No one said a thing, all just looking back at him with expressions that seemed even bleaker than before. They looked like Shane felt when he found out the government was responsible for killing his father and his aunt. Shane felt a surge of anger and sadness well up in him, and he gritted his teeth to keep it from showing on his face.

"Y'all know what Shamus and his gang are capable of, and they don't want the weapon shut down," Maurice said, breaking the gloomy silence. "We need people brave enough to fight and not afraid to die." He looked around. "If you're willing to go with us, stay where you are. If you're not, you best head back up the street and put some distance between yourselves and the fighting that's about to go down." Maurice pointed away from Shamus' territory.

Shane held his breath, looking at the somber faces. No one moved for what seemed like an eternity, and Shane became excited at the thought that all these kids were going to help. But then, a tall and skinny kid with dark hair and pale skin turned and walked up the street. One by one, other kids looked down at their feet, as if too ashamed to look at Maurice, and turned away, following the lanky, pale boy. Shane's hope faded as he watched the would-be army dwindle.

Chapter Thirty

Ten horrible minutes passed before the last of the kids unwilling to fight headed up the block. Shane surveyed those who remained, guessing there were at least fifty of them. Looking at their sad expressions, he wondered how many decided to fight because of bravery and how many because they didn't care if they lived or died.

"Alright, let's head back to the hotel and grab all the weapons we can carry," Maurice said, and then marched across the street and into the alley.

The group parted to let him pass, and then followed him, forming a long line.

"We'll be able to make it to the capitol with these kids helping us for sure," Kelly said. "Won't we?" Her wide eyes looked relieved, but something else seemed to stir in them—a sort of wildness Shane had never seen before. He feared the weapon was starting to affect her brain.

"Yeah," he replied, trying to sound as optimistic as he could. "We'll make it downtown without a problem." He put his arm through hers and tugged her along behind Tracy, who followed the last of their new friends into the shadowy alley.

They walked four blocks and entered a hotel with stacks of food and weapons lining the walls of the dark lobby.

"What happened to the lights, Jules?" Maurice asked a wiry girl with a mullet haircut.

"Don't know," the girl replied, chewing on a piece of gum and eyeing Shane and his flak-jacket-and-army-helmet wearing group with suspicion. "Lost power a few hours ago. Seems to be out everywhere."

"Oh wow," Maurice replied, scratching his head. "That sucks."

"Actually," Tracy interrupted, "it could be to our advantage."

"How's that?" Shane asked, glad Tracy was forming a strategy.

"If we head downtown after dark, it'll be harder for Shamus' gang to see us without the streetlights working," she replied, taking her green combat helmet off and holding it under her arm like a football.

"Shouldn't we leave now?" Shane said, afraid Kelly wouldn't make it to nightfall.

"No, she's right," Maurice answered. "We'll do a lot better under the cover of darkness." He glanced at Jules, who wore a look of confusion on her face.

"What's this about us going downtown and confronting Shamus?" Jules asked, sounding more curious than worried.

"I'll explain everything later," Maurice replied. "Take these guys to some rooms so they can get cleaned up and get some rest." Turning back to Shane, he said, "It'll be dark in three hours, then we'll leave. If you guys get a couple of hours of sleep, you'll do a hell of a lot better in the fight."

As much as he feared for Kelly's safety, Shane knew Maurice and Tracy's logic made sense. He looked at Kelly and then the rest of his group. They all had heavy bags under their eyes, like they hadn't slept in years.

"Alright," Shane said to Jules, "lead the way."

They followed the tall, wiry girl, who wore boys' blue jeans, a white T-shirt, and a black leather vest, through the hotel lobby and down the hall.

"This suite hasn't been used yet." Jules opened the door with a key card. "A continental breakfast will be served in the morning," she added with a comical voice. "Please enjoy your stay."

"Thanks," Tracy replied, sounding a little nicer than usual.

Jules smiled at Tracy and bowed, extending her hand into the suite.

"This place is as big as a house," Aaron said, walking into the main living area.

The rooms had large windows overlooking a garden area, allowing in plenty of light.

"There are two bathrooms—one for girls and one for boys," Kelly said, and then looked at Tracy. "Mind if I go first?"

Tracy plopped down on the couch in the living room and sighed. "Be my guest."

"You first in the boys' room, boss," Steve said, sighing. He clapped his hand on Shane's back.

"Thanks," Shane replied, uncertain as to how he felt to be officially labeled as the leader by Steve.

Too exhausted to give it much thought, he went into the bathroom and showered. He came out with a towel wrapped around him and slipped his pants on. There was a soft knock at the door.

"It's not locked—come on in." Shane sat down and then lay back on the bed, struggling to keep his eyes open.

Kelly opened the door, came into the bedroom, and shut it behind her. She had on a clean T-shirt and blue jeans, and her long, blonde hair hung straight and wet down past her shoulders. Shane had seen her dolled up at school and in a disheveled mess over the last few days, but he'd never seen her fresh out of the shower. He felt warmth stirring in his chest, and his face got hot.

"Mind if I sleep in here with you?" she asked with a timid voice.

"Uh…" Shane stuttered. "Sure—I don't mind."

"I don't mean to make you feel weird," she said, glancing down at her bare feet. "It's just that Aaron fell asleep in the other bedroom, and Tracy and Steve took the couches."

Shane patted the bed, trying to act casual, though he felt a little giddy from the idea of her lying near him. "One word of warning," he said, trying to ease the awkwardness, "I've been told I snore like a freight train."

Kelly chuckled and climbed into bed. She pulled the blanket and sheets out from under him, covering them both. Shane lay still and closed his eyes. Trying to be respectful, he made sure to keep to his side of the bed, though every fiber of his being wanted to roll over and put his arms around her.

"Are you scared, Shane?" Kelly whispered, her sweet breath warm on his cheek.

"Yeah, I suppose I am," Shane replied. "I mean, who wouldn't be?"

"You seem so confident… so sure that we'll make it downtown and shut the weapon off," Kelly said, her voice shaky. "You don't seem scared at all."

"I guess I'm just trying to hold it together the best I can." Shane felt his face getting hot from Kelly's compliment.

"I'm so scared," Kelly said, inching closer to him. "I know it sounds strange, but I feel like my mind is being taken over, like I'm losing myself."

Shane feared it was because of the weapon. Kelly slid next to him, pressing into his body. She pulled his arm around her and laid her head on his shoulder. Her hair smelled flowery and clean from the hotel shampoo. Shane wrapped his other arm over her and pressed his lips to her forehead.

"You're just exhausted," Shane said, trying to use a calm voice, though his heart raced and he was short of breath from her nearness. "Get some rest, and you'll feel better."

"You're probably right," Kelly replied, her eyes closing. "Can you promise me something?"

"Sure—anything."

"If I don't make it, promise me you'll go back and make sure Natalie is okay." Kelly's voice faded, sounding like she was half asleep.

"I promise," Shane replied, combing the hair out of her face. "But you're going to make it, so that won't be necessary."

The sound of her heavy breathing told Shane she'd drifted off. He looked up at the ceiling, still holding her tight in his arms. A few days ago, he'd have given anything to lie next to her and hold her like this, never imagining it would ever happen. It was like one of his wildest fantasies had come true, but unfortunately, in the middle of his worst nightmare. He wondered what it would be like to be this close to her under happier circumstances, hoping they survived so he might find out.

CHAPTER
THIRTY-ONE

A knock on the door woke Shane with a start. The sun had set, and thick darkness engulfed the room.

"Yeah," Shane yelled, hating he had to get out of the comfortable hotel bed. He felt like he'd just fallen asleep and, with Kelly pressed against him, he wanted to stay where he was forever.

The door opened, and a flashlight shined in.

"You two lovebirds ready to roll?" Steve teased.

Aggravated and irritable, Shane almost objected to being called lovebirds, but Kelly spoke before he had a chance.

"We're coming," Kelly said through a yawn, climbing off the bed and stretching.

That she didn't retaliate to Steve's comment sent heat surging through his body all over again. Shaking off the embarrassing surge of emotion, Shane got up, feeling like the short nap made him sleepier instead of refreshing him.

They followed Steve out into the living room, which was lit up by a battery-powered lantern sitting on the coffee table. Jules waited by the front door, her arms crossed and her expression impatient. Shane and Kelly slipped on their body armor and helmets, and then Aaron handed them their guns. The cold metal of the M-16's stalk in Shane's hands brought the reality of the battle they would soon face to the surface.

He glanced at Kelly, remembering the tender moment they'd shared a couple of hours ago, and how it seemed like the weapon was starting to affect her mind. Shane was scared fully awake, knowing he had to keep her safe—had to shut down the weapon before it got to her.

"Follow me," Jules said, then turned and led the way out of the room, down the hall and into the lobby.

Kids milled around the lobby, filling their backpacks with extra ammo and supplies and loading their guns. A cloud of excitement and dread amplified the tension in the room. Jules led Shane and his group over to a couple of tables set up with food. Shane picked up a sandwich and a soda, taking a big bite. His nerves were winding tighter by the second, and he didn't have much of an appetite, but he knew he'd need the energy so he forced the sandwich down as fast as he could.

"You guys get some rest?" Maurice asked, walking across the lobby toward them.

"A little," Tracy replied, sounding annoyed by his concern, like the business at hand was far more important. "Are your people ready?"

"They're all on edge," Maurice said, glancing around the lobby. "But they'll be fine."

Jules provided backpacks with water bottles and snacks for each member of Shane's team. Tracy split the remaining M-16 clips between them, and Shane stuffed the six she gave him into his pack. Trying not to worry they'd run out of ammo before they made it to the capitol, he put the backpack on and slung his gun over his shoulder. Walking over to the busted-out glass that was once the front entrance to the hotel, he gazed out into the darkness.

He remembered his football coach telling him a team could only be as strong as its leader. These kids would be looking for an example of courage and aggression. Maurice seemed to be a natural leader, and Shane wasn't sure he could do any better. But he couldn't leave Kelly's or any of his other friends' safety in the hands of a stranger. Whether he liked it or not, Shane had to take charge of these kids and lead them downtown. He took a deep breath, trying to channel Coach Rice one more time. He turned around, facing the kids scattered across the lobby.

"Alright people," he boomed. They all stopped chattering and turned toward him, eyes wide with anticipation. "We got a hell of a fight ahead of us, but we have the advantage. Shamus' gang fights for the sake of fighting—they have nothing to live for. We fight for our little brothers and our sisters. We fight to protect those we love," Shane glanced at Kelly, "so we cannot lose."

The kids stared at him, as if waiting for him to say something else. Shane had run out of words, and he hoped they'd cheer and rush out of the building into battle—like the football team heading onto the field. Of course, this wasn't a game. Shane could tell by the frightened looks on their faces that they knew many of them would die on this dreaded night.

"Let's go!" Shane shouted, pivoting on his heel.

He hoped the kids would stand up and follow him, but he didn't dare look back to find out if they did. He knew he couldn't show any hesitation, and he'd fight his way downtown by himself if they didn't join him anyway. There was no turning back for Shane—he was going to shut the weapon down or die trying.

"You heard the man," Maurice said with a booming voice behind him. "On your feet—let's do this."

A rustling and a wave of chatter followed. When Shane turned down the sidewalk, Kelly stepped to his right side and Aaron on his left. He dared a glance over his shoulder and saw Tracy and Steve behind him. Maurice's people spilled out of the hotel and fell in after Shane's brave little group, following them down the street.

They'd gone a block, weaving around car accidents and stepping over the bloated carcasses of adults, when Shane heard Maurice yell at the chattering mob, "Keep quiet! We don't want them to hear us coming."

A moment later, Maurice jogged up and walked next to Shane. He carried his black shotgun and had two pistols strapped to his waist that looked like the type the police used.

"While I admire your general badassness in leading us into the fight, we can't have you guys marching into Shamus' teeth at the head of the group," Maurice said.

Shane looked at him, surprised by the comment. "What do you mean?"

"Well, you guys are the only ones who know how to shut off this super weapon that's downtown, right?"

"Yeah—I suppose so," Shane replied, not slowing his

urgent pace.

"So we need to get you past Shamus' gang alive, so you can do what you got to do," Maurice said, his tone saying it should be obvious.

"What do you propose?" It relieved Shane that Maurice was thinking on his feet and acting like the leader Shane suspected he might be.

"I say we have my people surround you, and then we'll push straight towards the capitol building. Once we're there, we can hold off Shamus' gang while you guys go inside and do your thing."

"Okay—sounds good," Shane replied. The stocky kid turned to go back to his group. "Hey Maurice," Shane said, stopping him.

"Yeah, what's up?"

"Thanks for helping us, man."

"I didn't think we had a choice," Maurice replied, flashing a smile.

Two minutes later, Maurice had passed through the crowd behind Shane and his friends. Shane heard the jovial kid telling everyone to turn off their flashlights and ordering some of them to run ahead and take up position in front of the group. Half of the mob ran forward on either side of Shane, more kids than he saw earlier when Maurice called for those brave enough to help at the parking structure. Shane realized, to his relief, Maurice must've gathered more recruits while he napped, and now he was surrounded by a small army of brave teenagers.

"We should cover the upper parts of the buildings on

either side," Tracy said, waving the barrel of her gun at the second floor of an office building they passed. "I'm betting they'll attack us from up there."

The wind kicked up, covering the noise of hundreds of feet pattering down the dark, five-lane street. Lightning flashed across the sky, and Shane worried they might have to deal with another tornado on top of all the daunting challenges already ahead of them. But other than the brewing storm, the city seemed quiet. Shane hoped Shamus' people had sought shelter and called it a night. So many lives would be saved if they could make it to the capitol building undetected.

A motorcycle engine roared to life down a side street to their right, followed by another to their left, shattering any chance they hadn't been noticed. The engines revved and then grew quieter, headed toward downtown. Shane guessed they were scouts who went to tell Shamus to prepare for the approaching assault.

"They've spotted us," Shane shouted, adrenaline pumping through his veins and sweat forming on his brow. "Brace yourselves, people."

CHAPTER THIRTY-TWO

The sound of shotguns cocking and safeties clicking off rippled through the crowd around Shane. Two blocks later, motorcycles zipped up and down streets parallel to the one he and his small army walked on. The number of whining motorbikes increased with each block—giant, angry hornets getting ready to attack. When Shane and his mob walked over the hill, he caught a view of flashlights and torches flickering ahead, undoubtedly a gang of Shamus' people forming to stop the invasion into their territory.

Shane could barely make out Maurice walking at the head of the pack with his shotgun pointed down such that he could raise it in an instant and fire if necessary. They made it to the bottom of the hill and approached the gang of thugs. A flash of lightning illuminated Shamus' tall, skinny form at the head of the pack of armed teenagers, which looked to be as many in number as Shane's new allies. Maurice raised his free hand and stopped the mob behind him a half block from Shamus.

"What are you preppies doing down in this neck of

the woods?" Shamus asked, shining his flashlight up from under his chin in a way that cast his eyes in shadows and reflected off his gold grill. The boy obviously had a flair for the dramatic—he looked like the devil.

"We're just passing through, Shamus," Maurice replied, his stern voice as deep and loud as the thunder, but still managing to be friendly and disarming. "Best if you move aside."

"You got them kids who tore through here in that armored car, blasting my people to bits, with you?"

"I don't see how who we've got with us is any of your business," Maurice replied, sounding so authoritative and intimidating that Shane was sure Shamus would back down. "Now step aside."

"Well, it is my business. You leave those kids with me, and I'll let you pass," Shamus offered, the threat clear in his voice.

"Ain't happening," Maurice replied, raising the barrel of his shotgun.

"Then we'll have to take them from you," Shamus yelled.

The thugs with torches and guns moved forward, shouting threats at Maurice and his gang.

"Stay tight," Maurice yelled over his shoulder. "Let's punch through these bastards."

The mob surrounding Shane and his friends surged, pushing them forward. When they encountered Shamus' gang and had to stop, guns started popping off, first one at a time and then in a barrage of explosions. Adrenaline pumped through Shane, and he raised his gun toward the building on the left side of the street. Pulling the trigger, Shane shot a boy who leaned out of a window, aiming his gun down into Maurice's gang. The kid fell to the street, dead before Shane even realized what he'd done.

There was no time for Shane to feel any remorse over killing the boy. Gun barrels flashed in the second floor windows of the building, and Maurice's people dropped all around him. Survival instincts taking over, Shane aimed and picked off the snipers as fast as he could, afraid they'd hit Kelly or one of his other friends if he paused for even an instant.

With the deafening noise of hundreds of guns going off and people dropping dead all around him, Shane felt disassociated from his body, like he watched a character in a video game and wasn't actually killing and couldn't be hurt. Kelly stood next to him, and Steve stood on the other side, their flashing barrels raised and waving back and forth like Shane's. When his clip went empty, he dropped it on the ground, reached around to his backpack, and retrieved another. Slamming it into the gun, he knew his ammo was dwindling, but there was no choice but to continue firing.

The mob surrounding Shane and his friends sidestepped down the street, pushing through Shamus' gang. Suddenly, the head of a boy walking in front of Shane snapped back in a most unnatural way. Something warm and wet splattered his face, and he realized the poor boy's skull had opened up. He fell against Shane, leaving a trail of hot blood on his bulletproof vest as he slipped down, collapsing dead on the ground.

Using his sleeve, Shane scraped the dead kid's brains off his face and pointed the M-16 up at the balcony where the barrel of a gun had just flashed. The flickering light illuminated a teenage girl with tight braids hanging from either side of her head. She held a rifle aimed at him. They only stared at each other for an instant, but it seemed like an eternity, long enough for Shane to feel horrible about pulling the trigger. Her gun barrel flashed again, and Shane saw another one of Maurice's people drop in front of him. Kicking himself for the lethal moment of hesitation, Shane fired a burst of rounds from his weapon, and the girl slumped down onto the balcony, her gun falling end over end to the street below.

"They're mowing us down," Maurice yelled. When the conflict started, Shane saw at least thirty kids between him and the stocky leader of the assault. Now he counted half that.

"We have to charge them," Shane yelled. "Run!"

The remainder of Maurice's people surged forward together, pressing into Shamus' gang. In the chaos of the charge, Shane ended up next to Maurice.

"Get back," Maurice shouted, stepping in front of him. "We have to keep you alive."

Shane ignored him, leveling his gun and switching it to automatic. He wasn't going to get stopped here, he was going to make it to the capitol building, and no amount of armed thugs was going to stop him. Seeing the flash of the enemy's guns and Maurice's people dropping dead beside him, Shane sprayed the kids blocking the road with bullets and rushed forward into the opening he created. Dropping to a knee, he fired at the armed teenagers again, cringing as he watched them die.

Something hit Shane in the side of the head, and he fell to the ground. Looking up, he saw Shamus, standing over him with the butt of his gun raised, about to smash Shane's skull. The skinny gangster bared his gold teeth in a vicious grin and raised the gun higher.

Seeming to come from nowhere and moving faster than Shane imagined the chunky boy could move, Maurice leapt over Shane and buried his shoulder into Shamus' gut, knocking the wiry teenager to the ground.

"I got him," Maurice yelled, pressing his knee into Shamus' throat. "*Go!*"

Kelly and Aaron caught up and helped Shane scramble to his feet. They charged into a thin area of the gang blocking the street with what remained of Maurice's people at their heels. Adrenaline masking the pain of his bruised skull, Shane kept shooting and running with Aaron and Tracy on his right side and Kelly and Steve on his left.

A block down the street, Shane couldn't find anyone left to shoot at. By some miracle, they'd made it past Shamus' thugs.

"They're on our tail," Tracy yelled, not giving Shane a chance to rejoice at their success.

Looking over his shoulder without stopping, Shane saw the torches and flashing guns moving in behind him. At least a third of Maurice's people had made it through the roadblock, running backwards and shooting their guns to slow down the advancing thugs.

"They won't be able to hold them off for very long," Aaron yelled.

"This is our chance," Shane said. "We have to get to the capitol, now!"

CHAPTER
THIRTY-THREE

Holding the M-16 across his chest, its barrel hot from the firefight, Shane took off at a sprint with his friends behind him. The sounds of battle faded as they distanced themselves from Shamus and his gang. They crossed an intersection, and Shane heard the buzz of motorcycles, racing down the side streets. Running even faster, he feared they would cut back and try to intercept him before he made it to the capitol building.

Halfway down the next block, his fear was confirmed. Four motorcycles slid around the corner and did wheelies as they accelerated toward Shane and his friends.

"Take them out," Tracy shouted, leveling her gun and shooting from her hip while still running down the street. Shane and the others did the same, hitting three of the riders, who dropped to the ground, their bikes veering off onto the sidewalk.

The fourth bike sped toward Shane, moving too fast for him to aim at the rider. Shane fired several shots and missed. He saw the long, dirty blade of a machete in the bike rider's hand, and then the motorcycle was upon him.

"Watch out!" Aaron yelled.

Aaron leapt in front of Shane, knocking him to the ground. The bike passed, its front tire grazing Shane's arm. Aaron buckled over, holding his stomach.

"Aaron?" Shane jumped to his feet, catching his friend before he collapsed.

Blood poured out from between Aaron's fingers, draining onto the asphalt.

"No," Kelly shrieked, standing on the other side of Aaron.

The motorcycle slowed and turned around. Kelly raised her gun and let out a pained scream. She unloaded her clip into the motorcycle's rider, and he dropped dead in the street, his bike falling on top of him.

Aaron folded over, holding his wound. Shane dropped his gun and eased him to the ground, laying his friend's head in his lap.

"Hang on, Aaron," Shane demanded. A flash of lightning revealed the gash running across Aaron's abdomen. Guts had spilled out of the wound, and Shane knew there was no way he could survive.

Steve held a flashlight over Aaron and Shane, his face slack and pale with shock. Tracy squatted down and ripped packs of gauze open with her teeth, dumping them onto Aaron's gaping laceration. The white cotton turned to blood red in an instant.

"How bad is it?" Aaron asked, groaning in pain.

"It's just a scratch, man," Shane said, stifling his tears.

"You're going to be fine."

"Lying bastard," Aaron replied, with a weak smile. He coughed, and blood spurted from his mouth. "Do me a favor?"

"Yeah," Shane said. "Anything."

"Get your asses to the capitol and shut that stupid weapon down."

"We will, man," Shane promised. "Why the hell did you have to jump out in front of me like that?"

"Hey man," Aaron said, his voice faint. "I got your back—you got mine. Right?"

"Yeah, right," Shane said, trying to smile.

Aaron grinned up at Shane, and then his face went slack, his head rolling to the side.

Tracy stuck two fingers on the side of Aaron's neck for a moment and then looked at Shane with apologetic eyes.

"He's gone," she said, and sat back on her heels, rubbing Aaron's blood off her hands onto her pant legs.

Shane leaned over, wrapping himself around Aaron's head. A pained moan erupted from deep within him, tears flooding out of his eyes.

"Come on, Shane," Tracy said with a firm voice. "We have to go."

"Damn it! I know," Shane snapped, sitting back. He carefully slipped Aaron off his lap and lowered his head to the bloody asphalt.

Kelly helped him to his feet, saying, "He was so brave. Let's keep your promise and get to the capitol building."

Maurice's gang came over the hill, getting pushed down the street by Shamus' mob. Shane looked at the two fighting groups of teenagers—the reality of how little time they had to make it to the capitol motivating him into action.

He cleared his throat and wiped his eyes.

"Let's go," he said, and then continued running down the street, his promise to Aaron and his desire to protect Kelly pushing him forward.

It began to rain, soaking Shane's face and hiding his tears. He could only hope Aaron had gone to a better place— that maybe he'd been reunited with his mother.

Shane and Aaron had been close friends since they were little, playing football in every league together from the time they were old enough to wear a jersey. As he ran, Shane's grief transformed into anger. He wanted to get even with the people responsible for Aaron's death but, in reality, it was the same people who killed his aunt and dad. And those people had to be dead too. Making it downtown and destroying the weapon was as close to revenge as he'd be able to get.

With rain coming down in blinding sheets and frequent flashes of lightning illuminating the way, they sprinted three more blocks, trying to put some distance between Shamus' gangsters and themselves. Shane's ribs hurt from the effort, and he feared he wouldn't be able to keep up the pace, but then Tracy pointed at a dark building up ahead with a round dome for a roof.

"There it is," she shouted. "We made it!"

The capitol building loomed in front of them, a gleaming, white symbol of the government that failed its people. Recharged by the idea that they were so close to success, Shane took the steps two at a time. At the top, he rushed forward and pushed through the doors. Motorcycles buzzed onto the street below. Shamus' thugs jump off them and ran up the steps behind Steve, Kelly, and Tracy.

"Get inside and block the doors," Tracy yelled.

But Shamus' thugs made it to the top of the flight of steps, across the concrete walkway right behind her, and one had his weapon pointed at her back.

"Tracy!" Shane yelled.

Her eyes went wide, like she read on his face that he saw she was about to get shot. Without warning, four of the older thugs stopped and turned their weapons toward each other. With a loud boom of their guns going off at once, they wiped each other out. Only five younger kids remained on the porch of the capitol, looking at each other and at Shane and his group with confused expressions.

"It must be happening," Tracy said. "The weapon is starting to affect younger people."

Shane looked over at Kelly. Her eyes glazed over, like she was hypnotized. She glanced at Shane, Tracy, and then Steve, perhaps assessing their age to determine if she should kill them. Then she walked toward the steps stiffly with her gun raised toward the fighting teenagers down in the street.

"Grab her," Shane ordered, rushing after Kelly.

CHAPTER THIRTY-FOUR

Steve and Shane took Kelly's arms, and Tracy pried the M-16 out of her hands. Her eyes stared straight ahead and her face was pale, like she had become a zombie.

"Kelly? Can you hear me?" Shane asked. His worst fears coming true, he waved his hand in front of her face, hoping to bring her out of the murderous daze.

When she didn't respond, they tried to turn her around. Without a change in her empty expression, she resisted, like every muscle in her body wanted to go down and kill the teens fighting in the street below. Steve and Shane had to lift her off the ground to get her to face the other way.

"Take her inside," Shane said to Steve.

Steve nodded and lifted Kelly in a bear hug. She kicked and clawed at him but didn't make a sound. He carried her between the large, limestone columns and into the dark building.

Turning around and looking at the five stunned kids from Shamus' gang who remained on the capitol's porch, Shane shouted, "Now do you get it? This weapon is going to kill us all if we don't stop it soon."

The kids, all boys who looked to be about fourteen or fifteen years old, glanced at each other and then back at Shane. Their faces were slack with shock, and they suddenly looked very young and innocent.

"You know how to stop it?" one of them asked, a mixture of fear and desperate hope clear in his voice.

"Yeah, but we have to keep the rest of your pals from killing us first," Shane replied, pointing his gun at the two mobs engaged in a shoot-out at the bottom of the capitol building's steps.

Only a small contingent of Maurice's people remained. One of Shamus' thugs must've dropped their torch, because the building across the street was on fire. It created enough light for Shane to see a flock of crows swoop out of the dark sky and attack a girl off to one side of Shamus' gang. He worried the animals would be coming after Kelly next.

"We'll hold them off," the boy said, shouldering the butt of his shotgun and aiming down the steps. "You go shut that thing down." The others followed his lead, turning their backs to Shane.

Grateful these guys had a handful of common sense, Shane spun around and rushed inside.

"Help me," Tracy called after Shane stepped through the doors and shut them behind him.

He rushed over and got behind a large, antique desk, helping her push it in front of the doors to block them. The emergency lights around the parameter of the room provided dim illumination, so they weren't fumbling around in total darkness.

"The stairs are over here," Steve said, carrying Kelly across the room. She kicked and fought him, her face still blank as if she were under some kind of deep hypnosis, but Steve was so big and strong that he didn't have trouble hanging onto her.

Pulling flashlights out of their packs, they made their way down the marble steps and into the basement of the building. A small plaque at the bottom of the steps had the words *Federal Offices* printed on it and an arrow pointing down a pitch-black hallway.

"That has to be it," Steve said and rushed down the hall.

They came to a door at the end of the hallway with *B101* painted on the glass, and Shane opened it and peered inside. The emergency lighting in the room illuminated bodies lying everywhere. Some suffered gunshot wounds and others had their heads smashed in, like they'd been killed with office equipment used as weapons of opportunity.

"Eew, this place stinks," Kelly said. "Where the heck are we?"

"Kelly, you're all right?" Shane asked. Overcome with relief, he turned his flashlight on her face. Steve released her, and she stood on her own two feet. She no longer attempted to escape.

"Yeah, I think I am," she replied, shielding her eyes. "I must've passed out for a minute."

"Maybe the weapon only makes her go all weird when she's near other older kids her age," Tracy observed. She walked to the opposite side of the office and studied a large, stainless-steel door that looked like the entrance to a vault.

A scurrying sound made Shane look down. A rat ran across the floor and jumped on Kelly's leg, sinking its teeth into her. Kelly screamed, and Shane kicked it off and stomped on its head.

"This means the animals and bugs are gonna come after me," Kelly said. She sounded frantic, and her face turned white with fear.

"Don't worry—we'll protect you," Shane said. He looked over at Tracy. "Can you get that door open?"

"Yeah," she grunted, pulling on the large, shiny handle. "It's unlocked."

Shane latched onto Kelly's arm and tugged her across the room, kicking another vicious rat along the way.

"Shut the door," he ordered once they were all inside.

Steve helped Tracy close them in the vault. Shane searched the floor for more rats, but didn't see any. The small room's metal walls had racks against them, each one stacked high with file boxes.

"This can't be it," Steve said, sounding distressed. "There's no way out of here besides that door."

Tracy walked over to the left wall and pulled on a rack of boxes. When nothing happened, she worked her way around the room. Realizing she might be onto something, Shane started at the opposite corner and did the same.

"Got it," Tracy announced a minute later.

The rack she pulled on swung away from the metal wall. Shining his flashlight on it, Shane could see the outline of a door. When he pushed on it, it swung inward, stopping halfway when it hit the body of a woman, laying facedown on the tunnel floor.

"You think she's the scientist who recorded the message?" Steve asked, standing over the body.

"Could be," Tracy replied. "She is wearing a lab coat." She reached down and grabbed the woman's arm, flipping her over onto her back. The dark-haired woman's face was bloated, one side of it flat from lying against the hard floor. "Yep—says Dr. Gunderson on her name tag."

"Looks like she got shot and dragged herself in here to try and shut the weapon down," Shane said, pointing his light at the trail of dried blood leading back into the capitol building.

The tunnel walls were made of cinder block, and the ceiling was a smooth, continuous arch of concrete. The air smelled dank and stale, with a hint of rotten meat that made Shane feel sick to his stomach. A large, black beetle scurried out of the darkness and headed straight for Kelly. She shrieked, and backed against the wall. Shane managed to step on the beetle before it got to her.

"More bugs will be coming after her," Tracy said, sounding overly casual as usual. "Rats too."

"No, really?" Steve said, glaring at Tracy to scold her for her insensitive tone. "I think she already realizes that."

"Look guys," Kelly said, sounding like she was trying to muster her courage. "I'm right here, so no need to talk about me in the third person, like I'm already gone or something." She shined her light down the tunnel. "Can we just get going now, please?"

"Yeah," Shane agreed. He stayed close to Kelly, and they headed into the darkness.

"Look up." Tracy shined her flashlight at a black sphere hanging from the ceiling. "Cameras."

"And they got juice," Steve pointed out. "See the red light on the backside?"

"What did the scientist say? The secret laboratory is protected by an automated weapons system?" Kelly pulled her M-16 up to her shoulder and aimed it into the darkness.

"I wonder what that even means," Steve said. "Like flying drones with laser beams or what?"

"I'm sure we'll find out soon enough," Tracy replied.

"Keep your eyes peeled for a door on the side walls," Shane ordered. "The recording said the battery compartment would be outside of the laboratory. If we can cut the power, this will all be over a whole lot quicker."

They walked along at a rapid pace, the sounds of their footsteps echoing off the concrete walls of the passageway. A small herd of spiders rushed out of the darkness toward Kelly. She screamed and jumped behind Shane. He, Steve, and Tracy stomped as fast as they could and managed to kill them all before they got to her.

"I wonder how deep we are underground?" Kelly said once they started walking again, obviously trying to calm herself by thinking out loud.

"I'd guess we're pretty deep," Steve answered, sounding like he shared her need for a distraction. "We started at least twenty feet below ground level, and the floor has been sloping down for—"

"Shhh!" Tracy put her hand up to stop everyone.

Shane held his breath and listened, looking at Tracy's wide eyes and worrying about what could have spooked her. The unnerving answer came in the form of a mechanical buzzing sound echoing from the dark tunnel up ahead.

CHAPTER THIRTY-FIVE

"Turn off your lights for a second," Shane whispered.

The others did as he told them. The ominous buzzing sound grew louder. It reminded Shane of a remote control car, but a chill ran across his body as he imagined what kind of deadly military toy might be approaching, prickling with missiles and machine guns and having no conscience to make it hesitate from using them. Staring into the dark tunnel ahead, Shane saw a dim, red light.

"I see it," Tracy said, clicking her flashlight back on.

"Turn it off," Steve hissed.

"Why?" Tracy asked. "It's probably some sort of automated robot that uses infrared cameras to see. We're only blinding ourselves by keeping the lights off. I'm betting it's connected to these overhead cameras too. Probably been watching us the entire time."

"What should we do?" Shane asked, resisting the urge to turn and run the other way.

"Fight," Kelly answered, dropping to her knee and aiming her gun down the tunnel. Even while afraid they all might die, Shane couldn't help but grin at how tough Kelly had gotten.

"Hold on," Tracy said, putting her hand on the barrel of Kelly's gun and pushing it down. "Maybe we can fake it out."

"How's that?" Steve asked, his wide eyes glued on the darkness ahead.

"People must come through this tunnel all the time," Tracy replied. "If it thinks we belong here, maybe it'll leave us alone."

"Sounds like a long shot," Shane said. "It's got to have some pretty advanced ways of identifying people. Let's be ready for a fight if it decides to attack."

"You guys lay low behind me, so it only has one target," Tracy said, seeming confident in her plan. "I'll try to trick it. If I fail, be ready to blast it into scrap metal."

Although impressed by Tracy's bravery, Shane hesitated, worried about losing another friend.

"You have to trust me," Tracy said, her voice softer as if she sensed his concern. "I got this." Her eyes were persuasive, but also filled with confidence.

There was no time to argue, he clapped his hand on her arm and squeezed.

"Just be careful."

She nodded, returning her attention to the tunnel. He joined Kelly fifteen feet behind. Steve followed him, and they kneeled down on either side of the shotgun-wielding cheerleader, raising their guns and taking aim past Tracy.

The buzzing grew louder until a three-foot-tall square robot resembling the Mars Rover appeared in the beam of Tracy's flashlight. It stopped, and a metal neck unfolded, raising what looked like six camera lenses of various sizes attached to a volleyball-size, stainless-steel orb. The metallic, spider-eyed head of the robot stopped about five feet off the ground and seemed to study Tracy.

"Good evening." A friendly voice came from the head, blue LEDs flashing under the eyes as it spoke. "Please identify yourself."

"Dr. Sara Gunderson, leading a repair crew," Tracy said. Her voice was confident and so convincing that Shane was certain the robot would believe her. "Move aside and let us pass."

"Please wait," the feminine voice said. "Activating voice recognition sequence." After a pause, the robot continued, "Please count to ten slowly."

Tracy did as the robot asked, her confident tone not wavering for an instant. When she finished, the robot stared at her motionlessly for a few seconds. Shane held his breath, optimistic that the drone would let them pass.

The robot's neck collapsed, its head lowering back down to its square body.

"Voice recognition has failed," the kind voice said. "Please return to the capitol building for confirmation of identity."

"We can't do that," Tracy said. "Clearly, you are malfunctioning. We have to make emergency repairs."

"I'm sorry," the voice replied. "I cannot let you pass. Please return to the capitol building for confirmation of identity. If you do not comply in five seconds, I am authorized to use deadly force." Two gun barrels rose up on either side of the metal cube. "Five, four, three—

"Kill it!" Tracy yelled, flinging herself to the sidewall of the tunnel.

The robot pivoted to follow her, its guns blazing. Shane pulled the trigger, his gun set to fully automatic. Bullets and fire puked out of the barrel and into the robot, the thunder of gunfire reverberating in the tunnel. Steve and Kelly shot the drone as well, and the combined force of their guns pushed the drone back. Within moments, they depleted their ammo, leaving the drone flipped up on its side, filled with holes and oozing red and green fluids.

Tracy dropped to the smooth, concrete floor, holding her right thigh and groaning. Shane rushed to her side, noticing the blood staining her pants.

"Okay, stupid plan," she said, grimacing. She put her hands on her thigh above the bullet hole in her pants. "That hurts like a son of a bitch."

Red lights began flashing overhead and a female voice, similar to the robot's but louder, repeated, "Intruder alert, intruder alert. All security personnel report to the capitol building access tunnel."

"Let me see it," he said, pulling her hands away.

"It's alright," Tracy replied through clenched teeth. "I think it just grazed me."

She pushed Shane away and looked down at her leg. Tracy grabbed the sides of her pant leg and tore her jeans away from her wound. A small hole with black, cauterized edges pierced the outside edge of her thigh, blood seeping out of it.

"Lucky me," Tracy said, like she'd been through this a thousand times. "Is there a hole on the back side of my leg?"

She leaned over so Shane could see the other side of her thigh. Where the bullet exited the wound was bigger, but the bleeding didn't look too bad.

"Yeah, there's a hole," Shane replied, worried.

"Good, it means the bullet isn't still in me. Get some alcohol out of my pack and pour it over the wounds, then wrap my leg in gauze," Tracy ordered, cringing from pain.

"Keep your guns pointed down the tunnel," Shane said to Kelly and Steve, searching through Tracy's pack for medical supplies. "In case more robots come after us."

Tracy winced when he poured the alcohol on her leg, but she held it together. Shane finished wrapping her leg as fast as he could, and Tracy stood, using her gun as a crutch.

"I ain't never met anybody as tough as you," Steve said to Tracy, his eyes gleaming with amazement.

"Enough with the ass kissing," she replied, sounding annoyed. "We have to keep moving."

"What do you think will happen now?" Shane asked, pointing at the flashing lights overhead.

"How should I know?" Tracy replied. "Maybe an army of those robots will come after us. You want to wait around and find out?"

Kelly shrieked behind them. Shane turned and saw four rats jump on her and bite at her calves. He swatted them off, and Steve punted them up the tunnel.

"Come on," Tracy shouted over the sound of the

intruder alarm.

Grabbing Kelly's arm, Shane ran next to her down the tunnel. Tracy limped along with surprising speed considering her fresh injury. Rats scurried out of the darkness, and Shane and Steve kicked them away from Kelly, who shrieked every time she saw one.

"It's getting worse," Steve said. "We won't be able to keep them off her for much longer."

"Shut up and keep running," Shane replied. He refused to lose Kelly like he lost his aunt.

They came to a widened area of the tunnel that had fifty-gallon drums lining one side. Tracy stopped and flipped one over. Spiders rushed out of the darkness behind them, climbed up Kelly's pant leg, and she screamed. Shane squatted down and helped her smack them away.

Tracy stepped back and fired five shots into the top of the barrel, punching holes in the metal. Then she kicked the lid off with her good leg.

"Put her inside," Tracy yelled.

"What?" Shane looked at her like she had gone mad.

"Do it." Tracy grabbed Kelly's arm and pulled her toward the barrel. "Get in, you'll be safe here."

Realizing what Tracy had in mind, Shane smacked the rest of the spiders clear and picked Kelly up.

"What are you doing?" Kelly started kicking him. "I'm not going in there."

"If you're in the barrel, the rats and bugs won't be able to get to you," Shane explained quickly. "You have to listen to us right now."

Her eyes looked wild and full of fear, but Kelly stopped fighting him.

"Squat down," Tracy ordered. "Steve, give me your shirt."

Without hesitating, Steve removed his green military flak jacket, then pulled off his shirt and handed it to Tracy. Kelly lowered herself in the barrel, and looked up at Shane one last time, her eyes desperate and pleading.

"You'll be safe in here," Shane promised, though it felt like he'd said it as much to convince himself as her. He reached in and squeezing her hand one last time.

Nudging Shane out of the way, Tracy draped Steve's shirt over the top of the open barrel before putting the lid back on. Shane worried the only way Kelly could get out was if someone opened the barrel from the outside. If they didn't come back for her, then she'd die, tortured by the sounds of rats trying to chew through the metal to get at her.

"The holes in the top will keep the rats out, and the shirt beneath will keep the bugs from getting to her for a while, but she'll still be able to breathe," Tracy explained, answering Shane's concerns.

Shane helped her use a large, round, metal clamp to lock the lid in place just as a horde of spiders and beetles crawled over the barrel, covering it so completely he could no longer see the metal.

"You okay in there?" Shane yelled, sweeping the top clear.

"Yeah, I'm okay," Kelly replied. He could hear the terror in her trembling voice. "But please hurry. I don't know how long I can take this."

"Don't worry, we'll be back in no time," Shane promised, sick from imagining the slow and horrible death she'd face if for some reason they couldn't return.

CHAPTER THIRTY-SIX

"We have to keep moving," Tracy said, turning and hobbling down the tunnel.

Shane glanced over his shoulder while they rushed away, leaving the barrel covered in spiders and encircled by rats with Kelly in it in total darkness.

"Shouldn't we have left her some water?" Shane stopped, about to turn back.

"Yeah, we probably should have," Tracy replied, sounding aggravated. She held one hand on her injured leg and limped along with her gun raised and pointed into the darkness ahead.

"Don't worry, we'll be back before she gets too thirsty," Steve said with more compassion than Tracy seemed capable of, putting a hand on Shane's shoulder. "We can't risk opening the barrel now with all those bugs trying to get to her."

Reluctantly moving on, Shane felt like he left a piece of himself behind. He'd come back for her, he vowed. He wouldn't let her die crunched up in that horrible, dark can.

A herd of rats, more than they could possibly have

fought off, scurried past them and ran up the tunnel toward Kelly.

"See," Tracy pointed out, her voice strained with pain, "she's definitely better off sealed in the barrel."

Steve jogged around a bend ahead of Tracy and Shane, and a deafening roar of gunfire erupted, the tunnel ahead lit up by muzzle flashes.

"Steve?" Shane yelled, rushing to the corner.

Cursing, Steve rolled back by Shane, and the gunfire stopped.

Leaning around the corner and shining his flashlight down the tunnel, Shane could see another door that looked like it led into a vault.

"That must be the entrance to the lab," Tracy whispered over his shoulder.

"Yeah," Shane replied, "and it's protected by some crazy-looking guns." He shined his light up at two guns with multiple rotating barrels pivoting back and forth as if scanning the tunnel.

"Mini-guns," Tracy said. "They must only shoot when someone gets a certain distance away."

The concrete floor and walls of the tunnel had fresh scars on them from where the guns had shot at Steve.

"How the heck did you get out of there alive?" Shane asked, looking back to make sure the big linebacker wasn't hit.

Steve's face had lost all color. "I don't have a freaking clue."

"Look," Tracy said, pointing toward a less-impressive metal door on the right side of the tunnel, about fifteen feet away from the vault door.

"You think that's the battery compartment?" Steve asked hopefully.

"It has to be," Shane answered. "But the scientist made it sound like it was less heavily protected than the lab."

A rat came out of the darkness behind them, screeched, and then bit into Tracy's shoe. She looked down at it, and then glanced up at Shane with a worried look on her face. She was in the eleventh grade as well, and was the same age as Shane, so he wasn't sure why the rat had attacked her instead of him. Tracy kicked the rat down the tunnel toward the lab door. The mini-guns pivoted toward it and fired a burst of rounds, turning the rodent into a bloody smudge on the floor.

"When's your birthday?" Shane asked once the guns stopped, his ears buzzing from the noise.

"July," Tracy answered, understanding in her eyes. "When's yours?"

"October," Shane replied.

They looked at Steve, and he said, "August."

Five spiders crawled out of the darkness toward Tracy, and she stomped on them before they could climb on her shoe.

"The weapon must be affecting us now," she said, sounding more nervous than Shane had ever heard her. Shining her flashlight on the floor around them, she added, "We have to get to that side door before we start trying to kill each other."

"Obviously," Shane snapped. Anger surged in him,

and he felt the urge to punch Tracy. He knew the weapon had started to tweak his brain. Biting his lip, he fought the aggressive impulses getting worse by the second.

Taking a deep breath, he said, "I'm going to try and shoot out those guns. You guys might want to stay back."

Steve and Tracy got behind him, and Shane leaned around the corner. Expecting either of them to go nuts and shoot him in the back at any moment, he took careful aim at the guns.

"Try to target the motor that makes them turn back and forth," Tracy whispered.

"I'm not stupid," he replied, then bit the side of his tongue, trying to suppress another wave of rage.

When the mini-gun closest to the battery room door panned to the left, Shane pulled the trigger. He fired a short burst of rounds into the black box under the gun, and it stopped. Before he jerked his head back and took cover, Shane saw both mini-guns return fire. The good one swept back and forth, covering the tunnel in bullets, but the one he'd hit pivoted over a smaller area, only hitting the floor and wall on the right side of the tunnel, opposite the metal door he hoped led to the battery compartment.

"One down, one to go," he said, glancing back at Tracy and Steve. He looked at their eyes and tried to discern if they struggled against the near uncontrollable rage he felt. They seemed fine, at least for the moment.

But then Steve snarled, "What the hell are you waiting for? Shoot the other one out before I shoot you."

"Chill, dirt bag," Shane said. Without a second thought,

he brought the stalk of his gun back into Steve's gut.

Buckling over, Steve fell onto his side. Lying on the tunnel floor, he raised the barrel of his gun, pointing it at Shane.

A flash of light exploded from Steve's M-16, and the cinderblock wall next to Shane's head erupted into a cloud of dust. Shane jumped to the side, his face stinging from bits of concrete that hit him.

"Stop!" Tracy yelled, stepping between them. "Get control of yourselves."

Steve lay motionless, his eyes wide with shock. Shane wiped away the blood that trickled down his cheek.

"Sorry, man," Steve said, dropping his gun and pushing it across the floor of the tunnel. "I feel like something is trying to take over my mind."

"Me too," Shane said, remorseful. "I didn't mean to hit you, bro."

"We're all falling apart," Tracy observed. Shane could see her jaw muscles rippling, like she gritted her teeth to keep from yelling. He expected the only reason she hadn't lost it yet was because God had run short on emotions when it came time for her to get her share. "Shane, get back over there and shoot out the other mini-gun."

CHAPTER
THIRTY-SEVEN

Crawling to the corner on his hands and knees, Shane took aim at the second mini-gun. He hit the box it sat on when the spinning barrel turned all the way to the left. The mini-gun swung toward him and fired a burst of rounds. Shane slid back just in time, but his M-16 caught a bullet in front of the trigger, knocking the gun out of his hands. It slid across the floor and slammed into the wall.

"Did you get it?" Tracy asked.

"I think so," Shane replied, looking at his hand. His wrist hurt from the impact, and his knuckle was busted open and bleeding, but his fingers still worked when he made a fist.

Peeking around the corner, Shane saw the mini-gun he'd just hit had stopped moving back and forth. He retrieved his gun and slid it across the floor to the right side of the tunnel, just below the access door to what he hoped was the battery room. The automated guns lowered their barrels and began shooting, but they didn't pivot, only spraying the left side of the tunnel.

Turning back to look at Tracy and Steve, Shane leaned

against the wall and said, "Yeah, I got it. But the mini-guns will still fire when we try to get to that door. We could be hit by a ricocheting bullet."

"*We could be hit by a ricocheting bullet,*" Steve repeated in a mocking voice. "You sound like such a wuss."

"Shut up, fat-ass," Shane said, turning toward Steve with his fists balled up.

Tracy stepped between them again. "Hold it together, damn it. I personally would rather get hit by a ricocheting bullet than have one of you lackeys kill me. Now let's try to get to the battery room door and shut this thing down before we lose it."

Shane resisted the overwhelming urge to pummel the scowl off Tracy's freckled face. But a dwindling part of him still realized the weapon in the laboratory at the end of the tunnel caused his anger. He latched onto those fading rational thoughts and turned his attention to getting to the battery room.

"We'll have to stay to the right," he said, peering around the corner.

"No need to state the obvious," Tracy said, pushing him from behind. "Just go."

Gritting his teeth to keep from attacking her, Shane leapt to the wall with the battery room door on it. Tracy and Steve followed.

They crept forward, and the mini-guns started firing, filling the left side of the narrow hallway with a torrent of bullets. The guns fired so many rounds in close succession that Shane couldn't hear the individual explosions as each bullet was shot. Instead, he heard a loud roar that made his ears feel like they might start bleeding. Dust and smoke filled the tunnel, and bits of concrete sprayed him. Shane turned around and pressed his stomach against the wall to protect his face. Slipping deeper in the tunnel, his hand found the battery room door.

The handle wouldn't turn—the door was locked. Coughing and choking on the thick dust and smoke, Shane felt behind him. Finding Tracy, he felt his way down her arm and to her gun. He couldn't see her, and the deafening noise from the mini-guns made it impossible for him to tell her his plan. When he tried to pull the gun from her hands, she resisted.

Cursing, Shane grabbed her free hand and pulled it in front of him. He put it on the door handle and felt Tracy pull down. Apparently realizing he planned to try and shoot out the lock on the door, Tracy pulled her hand back and shoved her gun in front of him.

Shane rested the barrel of the gun on the door just in front of the door handle and pulled the trigger. The gun bucked in his hands, and the blast knocked the barrel hard to the left. When he went to try the door, a sharp, hot piece of metal cut his finger, but the door lock hadn't been broken. He wiped the blood on his shirt and stuck the barrel of the gun to the door latch again. Choking on dust and frustrated to the point of madness, he unloaded half of the M-16's clip into the door.

He pulled the gun away, and the door swung outward. Leaping through it, Shane gasped at the clear, albeit musty air.

He wiped his eyes clean and saw a large room, lit by a row of fluorescent lights hanging from the low ceiling. The center of the room was filled with giant, black, plastic blocks, standing up to Shane's chin and with thick wires hopping from one to the next on top of them. Only the twenty-foot-by-twenty-foot open area near the exit from the room where Shane stood and a small walkway around the perimeter of the big, black blocks was clear.

"Those look like batteries! This has to be the power supply," Shane said, turning around to look at Tracy and Steve.

Dust billowed in through the door, and the mini-guns still roared outside. But Tracy and Steve had yet to come into the battery room.

Fearing that they'd been hit by ricocheting bullets or concrete shrapnel, Shane held his breath so he wouldn't suck in any more dust and rushed to the door. He stuck his arm out and reached back up the tunnel to where Tracy had been standing. Feeling only the concrete wall, he groped down toward the floor and found someone's back. Shane grabbed his friend under the armpits and pulled. Once in the battery room, he saw he'd fished Tracy out of the choking cloud of dust. Her lower back had an area surrounding a tear in her shirt that was red, wet, and growing larger.

"You're bleeding!" Shane said, fearing she'd been hit by a stray bullet.

"Steve stabbed me," Tracy replied, grimacing as she pushed up onto her knees. "He must've hit a rib; I don't think the blade went very deep. You'd better watch yourself. He's lost it."

The mini-guns stopped firing, but Shane could still hear the whining sound of their motors spinning. They must have depleted their ammunition. He picked up Tracy's gun and pointed it at the door, worried that Steve would leap out of the dust-filled tunnel, and he'd have to shoot him.

"At least those damn mini-guns finally ran out of bullets," Tracy said, glancing out at the hall. Reaching back and putting a hand over her wound, she grabbed Shane's arm and pulled herself up.

"Maybe you should just stay down," Shane said.

"No, we have to shut this thing off." She hobbled to the batteries and leaned on them. "You guard the door. I'll find a way to cut the power."

Shane glanced at her and in an instant, he decided the right thing to do would be to shoot her and put her out of her misery. She probably wouldn't live very long with that hole in her back anyway, and she had to feel miserable after being shot in the leg and now stabbed. He raised the gun and took aim at Tracy's head.

CHAPTER
THIRTY-EIGHT

"Shane?" Tracy said, squinting her eyes in anticipation of the bullet hitting her. "You don't want to kill me." She had a calm tone to her voice, surprising considering she was about to die. "Lower your gun, please."

His finger moving toward the trigger, Shane replied, "I'm just putting you out of your misery. It's no big deal, you'll only hurt for an instant and then all the pain will go away."

"Listen to yourself," Tracy said, stepping toward the passage leading down the side of the batteries. "This is not you speaking, Shane. The weapon is making you crazy."

For an instant, Shane realized she might be right. He lowered the barrel of the gun a few inches, and a look of relief came over Tracy's face. But then again, he thought, she had been severely injured—she didn't know what was best for her at the moment. Shane raised the gun again and took aim. Tracy had made it to the corner of the batteries, but he could still easily hit her.

"Goodbye, Tracy," Shane said, and squeezed the trigger.

Just before the gun went off, something hit Shane in the back of the head. His bullet missed its target, slamming into the large battery just to Tracy's right. Stunned by the blow, he stumbled forward and tripped. He fell to the hard, concrete floor and rolled over onto his back. Steve leapt across the room and raised his gun over Shane's head. He drove the butt down at Shane, trying to smash his face.

Rolling to the side, Shane got out of the way just in time, the hard, plastic butt of Steve's gun making a loud thump on the floor an inch from Shane's skull. He rolled back and wrapped himself around Steve's legs. Twisting his body, he knocked him off his feet. Then Shane jumped on top of Steve and punched him in the face. Murderous hate and anger swelling in him, Shane punched with his left fist, then his right, hitting Steve so hard that his knuckles ached.

Blood splattered from Steve's nose, and the skin under his eyes split open. Shane hit him again and again, wanting to punch his face off, to see his brains underneath. Steve's legs came up, his knees pressing into Shane's midsection. Then he kicked and knocked Shane off him.

After tumbling back and slamming into the batteries, Shane leapt up. Steve was on his feet as well. The light glinted off the long blade of the hunting knife he held in his hand.

"Is that what you stabbed Tracy with, you bastard?" Shane snarled.

"Yeah, and it's what I'm gonna stab you with too," Steve said, smiling wickedly as he lunged forward.

Sidestepping the blade, Shane brought his knee up and pushed Steve's back down at same time. Steve grunted when Shane's knee sunk into his stomach. Shane dropped his elbow on the back of Steve's neck and knocked him to the floor. Moving surprisingly fast for such a big guy, Steve rolled away and came to his feet with the knife keeping Shane from closing in for another assault.

"Come on, punk," Shane taunted, "is that all you got?"

"No," Steve replied, wiping the blood off his nose with his free hand. "I'm just getting started."

He flipped the knife over so it pointed down. Raising the weapon over his head, he came at Shane again, stabbing at Shane from above. Shane blocked with his right arm, and the razor-sharp blade sunk into his flesh. He shrieked in pain and kicked Steve in the balls as hard as he could.

Steve backed away, holding the knife up to defend himself, as he folded over with his other hand on his crotch.

Looking at his arm, Shane could see the he'd been cut nearly to the bone. He cradled the wound and retreated to the other side of the room. Picking up the gun with his good arm, he charged Steve and swung the weapon like a bat. Steve ducked and swept his leg, knocking Shane's feet out from under him.

"Five years of tae kwon do, baby," Steve announced, jumping on top of Shane.

Steve stabbed down at Shane's chest, and Shane caught his wrist in both hands. His injured forearm felt like hot lava poured over it. He groaned loudly and tried to push Steve off, but he didn't have the strength.

Eyes filling with murderous hate like Shane had never seen, Steve put all his weight on top of the hilt of the knife and pushed down. Shane's arms trembled, his muscles giving out. The pointed tip of the knife eased toward his chest. A wicked smile crossed Steve's face. The knife pressed into Shane's shirt, first causing a dull pressure and then a sharp pain as it pierced the skin over his heart.

"Arrgh," Shane yelled. "Get off me!" In one last explosion of strength, he pushed the knife to his left.

The tip of the blade sliced across his chest, and it slipped down into his shoulder. Screaming in agony, Shane raised his knees and managed to push Steve up over his head. Shane slid his body out from under Steve and rolled away until he hit a wall.

Shane brought himself up onto his knees, cradling his bloody shoulder in his hand. He looked up in time to see Steve charging across the room, the knife raised and ready to deliver the final blow. Raising his good arm for protection, Shane dodged to the right, and the lights when out, the battery room cast in absolute darkness.

CHAPTER THIRTY-NINE

Shane crawled across the dark room and collapsed, huffing for air. He felt different—the pain from his injuries more pronounced, but his mind clearer. An instant ago, he hated Steve so much that he wanted to kill him and was certain killing Tracy was in her best interest as well. Now, he couldn't figure out why they were fighting.

"Shane?" Steve's concerned voice came out of the darkness. "Holy crap, man. Are you alright?"

"I'm a little busted up," Shane admitted, grimacing from the pain in his left arm and shoulder. "But I think I'll live."

The battery room and the tunnel outside were silent. The mini-guns' motors had stopped spinning.

"What the heck happened?" Steve asked, sounding like he'd just woken up.

"I think we just tried to kill each other," Shane replied, leaning against the cold, cinderblock wall and waiting for the world to stop spinning.

A flashlight at the far end of the passageway leading

down the side of the massive block of batteries flickered as it approached. Shane realized it was Tracy, moving slow because of her injuries.

"Tracy?" he called.

"I think I shut it down," she replied, her voice weak.

"Thank God—I almost killed you both," Steve said, his voice heavy with remorse and guilt.

"Don't give yourself so much credit," Tracy replied. "I was on my way back to kick your butt if the weapon didn't shut off."

"Tracy," Shane said, a relieved smile rising on his face in spite of his pain, "did you just make a joke?"

"Don't worry," she replied, stopping at the corner of the batteries and shining her light on her grinning face. "I won't let it happen again."

Tracy turned her light at Shane, and he squinted and looked down at his bloody chest. He had a nasty gash, and his arm didn't look any better. But at least the bleeding was slow, and nothing vital seemed to have been hit. When Tracy turned the beam on Steve, Shane saw his face had swollen and turned purple. Blood trickled out of his crooked nose and from the gash under his right eye.

"You guys look like crap," Tracy observed. "I hope you can walk, because I sure as heck ain't carrying you."

After Tracy used the remaining antiseptic and gauze from her backpack to dress Shane's wounds, he pushed up to his feet. He was dizzy from the pain and from losing so much blood, but he was able to stay upright. They worked their way into the tunnel, wrapping their arms around each other for support.

"Let's get out of here," Shane said, anxious to see Kelly and to breathe fresh air.

They made their way up the tunnel and toward the alcove where Kelly waited in her barrel. Too shocked and exhausted by the ordeal they'd just endured, Shane didn't say a word the entire way, and neither did his two friends. Was it even over? He couldn't believe the nightmare ended so abruptly. Maybe Steve whacked him on the head, sending him to this fantasyland of sudden peace.

"Kelly?" Shane called as soon as the barrel was in sight.

He slipped from Steve and Tracy's arms, fighting off a surge of pain. The fear that she may have died while they were away spurred him to a trot, making him ignore his discomfort. If the barrel had become her coffin, then all his efforts were in vain and he'd want nothing more than to join her in the grave.

Kelly's muffled response washed away his nauseating fear. Hope ignited in him with such intensity that it made the dark tunnel seem brighter. Shane rushed to the barrel and pried the lid off. The spiders and rats that attacked her before were gone.

Shane tossed the metal lid to the side, and it made a loud, clanking sound that echoed in the darkness.

"Did you do it?" Kelly gasped. Tracy's flashlight revealed a sweaty face covered in dirt, and eyes bloodshot from crying.

"Yeah—we shut it down," Shane replied, tears flowing. He reached in with his good arm and helped her stand. She was the most beautiful thing he'd ever seen.

Kelly hugged Shane, weeping joyously.

"Ouch," Shane groaned.

She leaned back and looked at him with concern. "Oh my gosh, what happened to you?"

Shane glanced at Steve, who smiled, his bloody mouth missing teeth. He shrugged his big shoulders in an innocent way.

Chuckling, Shane turned to Kelly. "I'll tell you later."

She looked at him with wide and worried eyes, then leaned forward and pressed her lips to his. In that moment, Shane forgot about all his pain and forgot Steve and Tracy probably stood there watching him with disgusted looks on their faces, letting the intoxicating bliss that came with kissing the hottest girl in school overtake him.

When Kelly pulled away, Shane and Steve helped her climb out of the barrel. They hurried as fast as their injuries would allow up the tunnel and through the capitol building. Walking out the front doors, Shane worried Shamus' gang might be waiting on them. Instead, Maurice slumped on the bottom of the capitol building's steps, his shotgun lying next to him. Morning had come, and the sky was miraculously clear, turning an inviting, soft blue color Shane had feared he'd never see again.

"What now?" Steve asked, spitting blood out of his mouth.

Shane looked around at the bodies of kids littering the steps, lawn, and the gardens of the capitol building, many of them several years younger than he was. It was the most depressing scene imaginable, somehow far sadder than all the adult dead he'd seen. He noticed a few kids down on the street below looking up at him. Maurice stood as well and waved at Shane and his friends, a weak smile and an expression of relief on his chubby and now much-younger looking face.

"We have to get back to the base and make sure my sister and the other kids are okay," Kelly replied, a desperate urgency in her tone.

"Yeah," Shane said. "And then we should get as far away from this city as possible."

He slipped his good arm around Kelly, and they climbed down the steps and across the wide, blood-covered concrete walkway to where Maurice stood. The sun peeked between the buildings and warmed Shane's face. Squinting at the brilliant light, Shane tilted his head back and looked up at the American flag dancing in the gentle morning breeze.

"Thank goodness you guys are alive," Maurice said, eyeing Shane's wounds with concern.

"Barely," Shane replied. "What happened to Shamus' gang?"

"I was out of it there for a while, but I guess most of the younger ones must've run off when the older kids started turning on each other," Maurice replied, looking at the street. He had a gash on his cheek, and his shoulders were slumped forward with fatigue. "I'm worried that they might come back at any moment."

"Yeah," Tracy said, staring down the street leading away from the capitol. "We should get out of here ASAP."

Steve picked up a motorcycle. "Come on, we can get back to the base a lot quicker on these," he said, pointing at several other abandoned bikes.

Maurice gathered the few of his people who survived and those who defected from Shamus' gang, and they climbed onto the motorcycles. Those too injured to drive rode on the back behind those who could. Shane sat behind Steve, Kelly rode with Maurice, and Tracy rode with Jules.

They buzzed up the street, leading away from the gold-domed capitol building just in time, because Shane glanced over his shoulder and saw some of Shamus' gang pull around the corner on motorcycles to give pursuit. After a couple of miles, the thugs seemed satisfied they had run the intruders out of their territory, and they stopped and turned back.

Every bump the motorcycle hit caused shockwaves of pain to flash from Shane's injuries and radiate throughout his body, but he managed to hang on and stay alert. When he wasn't distracted by the pain, the faces of all those he'd seen die and those he'd killed tormented his thoughts. He wondered if his mind would ever be at peace again, and expected to be plagued by nightmares whenever he finally had a chance to get some sleep.

By midmorning, they pulled into the military base. Kelly leapt off the back of the bike she rode on before it came to a complete stop and ran to the crowd of kids gathered around the lean-to shelters. Nat rushed out of the group, passing through the teenage girls who held their guns ready to defend the children against the approaching motorcycles. Kelly scooped her little sister up and held her in her arms.

"Where's Laura?" Shane asked, after he'd climbed off

the bike and limped to the girls who stood guard.

"She's over there," Rebecca, the red-haired girl who'd been assaulted in the gym replied, pointing at the cot that was used for Matt two days before. "A bunch of birds attacked her. We did our best to keep them off, but they cut her up pretty bad. Luckily, they stopped as suddenly as they started. A minute more, and I think she would've been killed."

Shane rushed to the cot as fast as his injuries would allow. Scratches covered Laura's face, and chunks of her black hair was missing, her scalp bloody where it had been ripped away. She had a makeshift patch covering one of her eyes, which Shane feared had been plucked out.

"Laura?" Shane gently touched her shoulder.

She opened her good eye, blinked, and then gave him a little smile. "You guys made it back," she whispered.

"Yeah, we did," Shane replied, trying to smile.

Laura began to push up to sitting, and when Shane tried to stop her, she said, "Don't worry, I'm not half as bad as I look. You guys must've shut that weapon down just in time."

"I suppose so," he said. Shane was relieved to see she wasn't dead or dying, but he knew by looking at her that her face would bear the scars of the bird attack for as long as she lived.

"I think we should head north," Tracy said. "It doesn't feel safe here, so close to the city. As soon as the bodies start rotting, the gangsters may start venturing out into the suburbs."

"You're right," Shane said, cringing at the pain that shot through his neck and shoulder when he glanced at her.

He reckoned, like Laura, they'd all have scars from the last few days for the rest of their lives—both inside and out. "Let's try to find some trucks to load these kids on and get the heck out of here."

CHAPTER FORTY

Proving to be quite the amateur doctor, Tracy recruited some of the healthier people to treat the wounded with the medical supplies they scavenged. She even found antibiotics and had those with deep cuts and gunshot wounds, including Shane, take them to prevent infection. Maurice and Steve acquired a couple of large military trucks in which everyone could ride. After gathering all the weapons they could carry, they drove away from Atlanta.

They visited every grocery and convenient store they saw along the way and loaded up on canned goods and other nonperishable supplies. Some of the stores had already been picked over, and they kept watch for other groups of kids roaming around north Georgia, but they didn't see any. Shane knew that when the grocery store food ran out, he'd need a way to provide for the kids for whom he and his friends were responsible, so he decided they should try to find a farm that could supply them with everything they needed.

That night they stopped in a rural area forty miles northeast of Leeville on a large farm. Seeing the cattle and other animals made Shane nervous, but they took no interest in him and his friends. The civil war-era mansion had plenty of room to sleep everyone and a generator out back got the power going. They all took showers and had a large meal with hardly a word spoken the entire time. Shane passed out on an old, musty couch in a hallway near the front door of the home, a half-eaten plate of food on his chest.

"Good morning," a woman's voice roused him.

Shane sat up, groping for his gun. Unable to find it, he raised his hands and blinked his eyes at the sun blazing through the open door. An adult—a woman in a black suit—stood in the doorway.

"What?" he bumbled. "How…?"

"Some of us survived," she explained.

The thumping of a helicopter wound down outside, and another one flew overhead.

"You guys are safe now," the woman said. She looked to be about thirty, a slender brunette with intelligence glistening in her eyes. "But you'll have to come with us."

The End—The Last Orphans Series Book I

ACKNOWLEDGEMENTS

As I think about who to thank for helping me in my journey as a writer and ultimately in the creation of this book, dozens of faces and names come to mind. Writing, and art in general, draws influence from life, and in life I've encountered so much inspiration each day. I am inspired by my fellow writers, my friends, my family, and even random strangers who spark my creativity just by being who they are. So, writing acknowledgements is a daunting task to say the least. An incomplete list of those who deserve recognition will have to do.

I want to thank my wife Amanda, who reads everything I write and cheers me on through the joys and tribulations of being a writer. Thanks to Emily and Logan, my beautiful children, who constantly remind me that we are born with imagination abound, that we just have to remember to listen to our inner child and creativity will come naturally.

Thanks to the amazing Clean Teen Publishing team. From the first interaction I had with you, I knew I was dealing with a rising star in the publishing industry. Thanks

Dyan Brown, Rebecca Gober, Marya Heiman, and Courtney Nuckels. From cover to cover, you helped me polish The Last Orphans and make it into the book it is today. And thanks to Cynthia Shepp, my editor, who found a home for orphaned commas, ironed out confusing sentences, and was always there, tirelessly helping with edits to the last detail.

Thanks to Jennifer Anne Davis, my writing partner from the beginning and my friend of many years. I am happy to follow in your footsteps and learn from your persistence and unwillingness to settle for anything short of success. Thanks to author Mary E. Pearson for believing in me and encouraging me to keep writing. And thank you Celso, Andy, and coffee shop Kevin, those early readers who had the patience to see past the crudeness of my rough drafts and offered enthusiastic encouragement. Also thanks to the beta readers at Clean Teen Publishing and Melanie Newton and the Clean Teen Publishing Street Team for reading and promoting my book—you are integral to the success of all CTP writers.

ABOUT THE AUTHOR

Born at the end of the Vietnam War and raised on a horse farm near small town north Georgia, N.W. Harris's imagination evolved under the swaying pines surrounding his family's log home. On summer days that were too hot, winter days that were too cold, and every night into the wee morning hours, he read books.

N.W. Harris published his first novel—Joshua's Tree—in 2013. It was no wonder that with his wild imagination and passion for all things word related, that N.W. Harris was named a quarter finalist in Amazon's Break Through Novel Award Contest. In early 2014, N.W. Harris joined the ranks with Clean Teen Publishing when they signed his new young adult apocalyptic adventure series—The Last Orphans.

In addition to writing, N.W. Harris has been a submarine sailor, nurse, and business owner. His studies have included biology, anthropology, and medicine at UCSB and SUNY Buffalo. He is an active member of SCBWI and lives in sunny southern California with his beautiful wife and two perfect children. He writes like he reads, constantly.